AN EXPERIENCE OF TERROR YOU MAY NEVER FORGET

THE HILLS
WINDSOR of

To Lexie —
Best Wishes
S M Quaranta

S. M. QUARANTA

BOOK ONE OF THE MAN IN THE MOON TRILOGY

Wasteland Press
www.wastelandpress.net
Shelbyville, KY USA

The Hills of Windsor
by S.M. Quaranta

First Printing – July 2017
ISBN: 978-1-68111-192-6

Printed in the U.S.A.

0   1   2   3   4

In memory of Rocco Quaranta

PART ONE:

Amber Snow

SUMMER 1935

ROSE CARLISLE CONSIDERED HERSELF CLAIRVOYANT, yet she had received no vision, not even the slightest premonition, of what that storm on the 17th day of August would bring. Likewise was the storm. Unannounced. It seemed to rage into Windsor's little river valley like a creek in spring thaw, ripping the bird nests from the grasses and the bark off the soft maple trees. There had been no sign of a storm in the sunset of the 16th. The animals showed only the most usual agitations, evidence that even the flies were being fooled.

Rose's husband was signed onto Cortland Snow's farm, giving him a split profit in the said farm and half of a twelve room house which had been converted for tenantship. They had been here for three months, 17 days, and a year before that. He was down by the river, at the south-east corner of the farm. Rose was trying to cool the kitchen she was just about finished baking in. It was seven o'clock, exactly seven o'clock because she was looking at the timer. Cortland would be on his way back for a supper that should have been at eight o'clock, drunk, but the horse knew the way home. (Course, Mrs. Snow was always in their prayers.) When the storm hit it shook the house. Rose's first concern was for the children. Her two boys were with her husband; but where were the girls? Amber had just recovered from the measles and little Edythe was bound to be frightened by the storm's fury.

There was a loud explosion when the lightning hit the house. Her son would find the lightning rod, along with the weather vane, later that day on the ground an acre away. In the kitchen electricity poured from an inoperative faucet, blackening the sink, raising welts in it. The patterned wallpaper around the telephone steamed before it was reduced to scorched, tattered curls. The lights blazed like holy Moses and they would not be turned off.

Rose hadn't moved a muscle since she looked at the timer. The inside of the house was hushed by a terrific wind outside. In spite of it, she heard Edythe's scream. Then she heard the fire in the house. She ran out, never thinking about taking an armful of valuables with her. For the rest of her life she'd mourn over the oil paintings done by her father, hanging—and she imagined them burning—on the parlor wall.

Outside she was nearly stopped by the shock of seeing little Edythe carrying her older sister toward the burning house. There was a look of relief in Edythe's round face as she was nearing the porch step. Rose stepped down to her and sank on her knees to the child's level.

"Lightnin' hit 'er!" yelled Edythe, still holding Amber.

"House is on fire," Rose told the seven-year-old. Edythe's face started to crumble but Rose slapped it. A lone tear escaped her eye and rolled around her right cheek.

"Take yer sister out away from the house and lay her in the grass." There was smoke in the wind, twisting about them in long arms. "I'm going for my son. Be right back."

She ran a bit and turned around. Confused, Edythe had taken a few steps toward her.

"Where?" cried Edythe.

"Away from the house. Up on the hill." Then Rose was off, screaming for anyone who would hear.

Edythe carried her sister back the way she came, falling twice, the second time loosing her shoe. She carried her down and up a drainage ditch and through the sassafras grove, yet she didn't stop. Across a small field she climbed an earthen mound, placing Amber down on top of it.

If Rose had known this she would have strongly objected, house ablaze or not. One year ago, in a spasm of clairvoyance, she perceived the mound to be wicked, or cursed, perhaps. After that, the girls were to stay away.

Maybe if the rain had come right away the house could have been saved. For a span of an hour, while Cortland Snow's farmhouse had become an inferno, hell's center, Edythe lay with her head on Amber's chest. Her sister had no heartbeat, not the whole time. There was a kind of absurd, paradoxical peace on the miniature hill. Later, when Rose's lengthy figure came into her tilted view, Edythe barely noticed how the woman hurried. Rose's expression, an outcry of her soul, horrified of some evil besides the fire, didn't quite register. Only then did Amber's heart begin again, struck by neither another thunderbolt nor the address of angel musicians. It was that face of horror that brought on the beat.

FIFTY YARDS FROM THE OLD A NEW HOUSE was being built. Rose Carlisle, her husband and their children had moved on, at Rose's insistence; she held that the Snow family was hexed and that the fire was only the meager beginning of misfortune. The barn would become a tenant's apartment and behind that was now the basis of a makeshift barn. Cortland's friends and drinking colleagues lent a hand in the construction. Edythe and Amber had spent the months with the O'Neal family, who'd lost two of their own children the year before in a drowning.

The weather had been the unusual, which was usual. Rain knocked down most of the leaves. Cortland brought his two girls up to the ill-fated farm so they could choose their pumpkins. The girls could hear, even from the pumpkin patch, the frantic pounding of hammers, like a swarm of woodpeckers. The ground was so soft that their shoes stuck under the vines. Edythe, holding a pumpkin to her belly, began to carefully carry it. Her sister wasn't much interested in the fat pumpkins and she wandered off.

It was her first time back after the storm had struck her down. Amber stared at the hole where her house used to be, at the ring of trampled black grass.

She didn't proceed right to the mound, she side-tracked along a stone wall and crossed the drainage ditch there. Now up the slight, tree studded hill and she found the path. And still she could smell soggy, acrid smoke if she wanted to, if she sniffed hard, but maybe it was her. Maybe a dark wisp of that smoke had clung and held to her. Soon the path turned a sharp left, taking her out of the woods, winding, snake-like. She ran forward, to the head of the snake; to the mound.

It was surrounded by thorny brush and small trees, yet the saplings that grew from its flanks were sparse, and the brush was not all that thick. She didn't know what she wanted to do first. Amber paced back and forth, until she finally settled on the mound like a cat on its master's lap.

She sang softly to herself as she strolled around the perimeter of the square mound. The song was one she'd heard Rose sing, though she wasn't sure that she had the words right and she hadn't heard the song in some time. It was an Indian song.

"Oh the moon shines tonight
On pretty red wings
The breeze is sighing
The night birds crying
While afar beneath the star
Her brave lies sleeping
While red wings weeping—"

A movement quieted her. It wasn't the ground for the mound itself was still except that it oozed rainwater like a sponge. The tremor was something *in* the ground, reminding her of a story about a big groundhog who woke up a few seasons late.

Later, she found Edythe in the shed. Her sister's pumpkins, five of them, were neatly arranged outside the open door in a row from biggest to smallest. One was cracked. Edythe must have dropped it.

"Wanna play Aunty Over?" Edythe asked her when she entered the shed.

"Need more players, idjot," Amber told her.

Amber's eyes moved about the shed, searching for something, her face blank. Edythe followed her as her older sister's eyes settled on metal stakes and shovels, pitchfork and sickle, harnesses and chain and augers and axes. When her eyes fell upon a fish spear—five feet long and strong and narrow—she paused. She lifted it carefully from the wall. After weighing it in her hands, she pointed the small spearhead at Edythe's throat. She jabbed. Edythe stepped back; as her heart skipped a beat she fell, her head only just missing the barbed point of the spear.

Amber left her sister sitting in a mess of chicken wire and returned to the mound. She began to poke the fish spear into soft, moist earth, picking a spot randomly. When the spear struck rock she pulled it out and tried again. After a few minutes she decided to start at one end of the mound and work her way systematically across the top, moving the spear about six inches each time she struck an obstacle beneath the soil.

She was getting bored and tired when, in the center of the mound near the place she had started, the spear sank half way with only a bit of difficulty. When she wiggled it, it sank lower.

She withdrew it, leaving a small hole. Parting the grass, she got on her hands and knees for a closer examination. Sucking on her lower lip in concentration, she stuck her finger in and encountered something cool and soft. It wriggled against her probing fingertip, seemingly feeling her as she felt it. She pulled out a broken earthworm.

A few inches from the finger sized hole she again stabbed the mound. The spear stuck. But a few inches in the other direction it slid in unobstructed. She left it protruding as high as the grass so she could easily find it later, and ran skipping to the new barn to brush her calf Yosemite.

ONE

Hilary did not enjoy her first impression, which usually she tried to savor. The house in Windsor showed much worse disrepair than she had realized or remembered. Or had all the deterioration happened during the fifteen years since she'd last visited? Anyway, she'd have to wait until morning; it was too dark to tell how bad it was. Hilary walked quickly to the house, clutching a bag and a suitcase in each hand. She tried not to acknowledge that there were bats above her; she had looked up toward the stars when she got out of the car and had seen them circling. As she approached the porch it looked as if something was perched on the roof. Just branches, Hilary told herself, though she couldn't remember if there were any large trees that close to the house.

Early Monday morning, Hilary's father had died of an unexpected heart attack in his store, a bakery which he'd maintained for forty-three years, and Hilary had accompanied the body from Albany to Windsor, arriving just an hour ago. She was tired. Each of the porch steps leaned at a different angle. The floor of the porch was warped and she nearly fell walking across it. The front door was thick and heavy; Hilary remembered she had trouble with it as a child. There was a porch light and she wondered why it wasn't on.

Standing at the door she wondered what to expect. What cherished childhood wonders waited to be erased? She tried to force her thoughts of Amber Snow, her grandmother's sister, to lean towards amusement rather than dread. Surely the insane old woman would be hopelessly—*hopefully*—senile and bedridden by now. But that was not fair, Hilary realized. Amber Snow had never been entirely insane. Her eyes, Hilary remembered, had been too clear for that, too crafty. And both women were too strong to ever succumb to a bed. Hilary couldn't make herself believe that fifty years, let alone fifteen, could change that.

As she hesitated, the door was swung open by Edythe Snow and at once, in a shock of smells and sights and sounds, Hilary Critchlow found herself to be twelve-years-old again instead of thirty.

They embraced. Hilary's chin rested on Edythe Snow's snowy white hair which was set in a massive snowdrift. A scent was in the air, something baking. Beneath that, the house smelled like sweets: cinnamon and licorice. Edythe took Hilary's bags and set them down on the bottom step of the staircase. Hilary sat down at the kitchen table, running her hand over its wooden surface, remembering sitting here half her lifetime ago. Suddenly she could identify the smell of pie seeping through the oven door. It was a gas oven that looked old; if it had been here when she was young, she couldn't recall it. It had been the wood stove in the front room that Hilary remembered. There used to be a rocking chair next to it from which Edythe had read her stories.

There was dead silence in the kitchen, broken only by the clink of the cups on saucers as her grandmother poured tea. Hilary's eyes brought her sleepy attention to a high corner shelf holding mixing bowls, but mostly holding shadows. It must have been fatigue that caused her to see a bearded head on the shelf. She closed her eyes and rubbed them. She was not going to let the strain of the drive from Albany effect her mood.

Edythe Snow was carefully carrying two ceramic mugs to the table when Hilary suddenly jerked fully awake.

All houses make noises, Hilary told herself. She had thought she heard the sound of stiff bristles against the back door. Walls can creak under the weight of a roof, she reminded herself. Windows sometimes snapped in their panes.

They talked for an hour, about where and when the funeral would be held, and about the burial in the family plot. Edythe was reminiscing how much she missed Hilary's childhood visits when she said:

"I think I forgot to turn on the porch light for you."

She abruptly stopped talking and placed a hand in the air, spotted palm out, as if to stop Hilary from moving before she had the chance.

"Haven't... talked this much... in ages."

Hilary didn't know whether she should help the old woman or not. And worse, she didn't know how. She waited, staring at Edythe's nearly transparent bluish and pink eyelids until they fluttered open. In Edythe's glassy eyes, Hilary saw no rationality.

"Amber!" Edythe cried with what was the exhale of the last difficult breath she had drawn. Her glistening eyes seemed to become as hard as smoky quartz. She seized her granddaughter's hand with frightful savageness. Hilary was too stunned to try and pull away.

She wasn't sure which to fear more, her grandmother's sudden seizure or the appearance of her great Aunt Amber.

"Is that you?" Edythe cried out, still staring hard at Hilary. There was noise upstairs.

All houses make noises. Hilary followed this one with her eyes across the ceiling. She had been meaning to ask her grandmother about Amber Snow from the moment she walked in the front door but had been afraid of the answer. What did she think it would be? That Amber Snow was dead? A chill like a blast of winter crawled up the back of her blouse. She wrenched her hand from her grandmother's grip, reached across the table, and tried to shake her grandmother out of her trance.

Edythe Snow's blue and pink eyelids slowly folded open then closed, and open then closed again, several times. Pie crust was burning in the oven, berry juices sizzled, sputtering like snakes on fire. The noises upstairs came to a halt near the top of the stairs.

Hilary's busy gaze moved from Edythe's gossamer, insufficient eyelids to the fuming gas oven, then over her shoulder, through the knotty-pine arch and into the front room.

She didn't think she could see the staircase from where she sat, until a swelling gray figure moving down an angled swath of darkness on the opposite wall revealed to her that the swath of darkness was the staircases shadow.

Hold on! Hilary's overwrought, tired mind began to call out. Back up one step and calmly take a look at what's going on!

Edythe had begun to breathe again, thank God. Hilary had no idea if it was the gentle shake that did it or just plain good luck. To her amazement, Edythe did not run, but moved rather quickly to the oven door and pulled it open.

"I'm fine, I'm fine," she repeated, tending to her blackened pie. Heat from the oven raised weedy strands of her white hair. Like embarrassment the air became abruptly hot.

Hilary stood up. She waited, awkwardly, while nothing happened. The heat from the oven slowly dissipated into the house. The silence unnerved her. Edythe nitpicked over her pie.

"Damn!" the old woman cursed.

"*Iknowyou.*"

In the same instant Hilary wished and prayed it was… and realized it wasn't, a cat. It sounded like a cat. Not a house cat, but feral.

"*Ido.*"

It was Amber who rarely spoke in discernible sentences. Oh, she had spoken clearly enough on several occasions, and Hilary remembered one such utterance right now. It popped like a bubble in the deepest tissues of her brain, splattering the words like it did every so often across the echo-chamber of her mind.

Lovey dovey in the dark.

How long ago had Aunt Amber said those words to her? It must have been more than twenty years now.

Amber Snow muttered somewhere in the house, only the muttering had lessened into a whine or a purr. Hilary caught Edythe's gaze darting over her shoulder towards the front room. She held herself from turning around. She could see in the old woman's eyes that so far the front room was empty. As she watched Edythe's eyes, they slowly unfocused. "*Little bitch,*" Edythe mumbled with a thick tongue. Hilary was shocked by the sound of her voice. "*The little—*"

Not again, Grandma, Hilary thought. Don't leave me alone again. It's only the first night in fifteen years. I have to get used to always *hearing* Aunt Amber about the house but rarely *seeing* her.

Edythe's head rocked slightly. Her face took on a puzzled look; her thin lips parted into an O, her eyebrows formed pale arches toward a hairline like a thinning gray forest.

"*I—don't—know!*" she cried and by her eyes Hilary could tell she cried only to herself.

Hilary watched as those eyes clouded, Edythe's pupils crowding with two rotund twin-images. Hilary looked closer, but her head blotted out the reflected image of Amber Snow. She would have to turn around now. She would have to see her aunt through her own eyes. Her grandmother's eyes were showing her a distorted Amber Snow. The convexity of her eyes was giving Amber a corpulent, fleshy appearance. Amber's midsection ballooned into a moon-shape, plump and heavy.

Because her gaze still looked inward, Edythe did not at first see her elderly sister. Not until Hilary began to turn around did she blink and become aware of what fell into the outer range of her vision.

"Shoo, fly, shoo!"

Hilary turned. She was momentarily struck dumb. Amber Snow looked horribly old—*How old is she*, Hilary thought, *ninety, ninety-five?* Her naked face and arms looked as tough as driftwood, and scorched to a crisp darkness by the sun.

But Hilary...

She turned, still. And tried to hush her mind.

Amber's midsection *was* ballooned. It hung distended in a way no garment could hide. That same section of the housedress she wore was stretched colorless and thread-bare.

She's... Hilary, she's...

Sho, fly, shoo!

But she had to concede, unwillingly. The old woman appeared to be—no, there was no doubt now, Hilary tried to doubt, but it didn't work. Amber Snow was expecting, she was... with child. She was pregnant.

HILARY STIFLED A CRAZY, HYSTERICAL LAUGH. She knew that it was hysterical because she couldn't squelch it in her mind. It screamed in a mad cackle. She swooned, felt faint.

There was a confrontation. The two old women shuffled in each others arms. Hilary gasped. She swallowed but her mouth contained no saliva. She fully expected the impossibility: that these two elderly sisters would fight... physically fight. Brittle fist to wrinkled face. Bloody gums and waxy purple bruises.

Edythe Snow wouldn't hurt a pregnant wom—

No, no, no. She isn't pregnant. Sick maybe. *A tumor?* But not pregnant she couldn't be pregnant never pregnant impossible.

The two old women, almost dancing, struggled around the corner.

Hilary waited; stood; hesitated; waited.

In time a bloated shadow moved up the other rooms wall. The dark, rounded shape appeared defeated. Tired and powerless.

Dying? Hilary wondered. Could Amber be dying?

She was waiting, something told her. Edythe had not looked fully in control. That shadow said just as plain as night and day, that it only waited.

TWO

HILARY CAME AWAKE as the sun came up and was greeted immediately by a nasty fever which reclined in her head, amusing itself by pounding long nails into crevasses in her skull. Her shoulders ached, her hands trembled beneath the sheet, her legs felt as if they were entirely missing and the only feeling she thought she could muster was a floating memory of them. Sitting upright, the weight of the fever leapt like a fat troll to her lap. Moaning, she rubbed at her face. When she stood at the side of the bed that same fat weight tried to pull her back down.

The room was small and painted a wilted yellow. There was just enough room to move around the two sides of the bed that weren't against a yellow wall. Three feet from the foot of the bed was a window with a broken pane; a tree branch scraped against the crack like a finger picking at a scab.

She dressed slowly, her head in pain at first but after a few minutes the pain subsided. As she ate the breakfast Edythe made her it nearly went away. Edythe was now much like the morning sun: bright and nothing less than cheery. She prepared breakfast in a way that only a grandmother can. Each egg was opened with tender care, each slice of toast was made as if they were the most precious of delicacies. The pancakes were perfection. Her home-made boysenberry syrup superb. It was as though the breakfast was a cure.

Hilary used force to get her way and wash the dishes. She did them as she had watched her grandmother doing them. She found that cleaning the countertops helped orient herself with the organization of the kitchen. Finally, as she finished cleaning up, Edythe seemed to settle into a chair at the table and relax, pulling her coffee to a suitable distance away from her bosom.

Hilary turned from the countertop, rubbing her hands lightly; they were slightly raw from the dish soap. Now, she felt, was time to be serious. Her fever and delirium were gone.

She decided she wouldn't bring up Edythe's attack last night, something in her memory told her that would be best. Hadn't she always suffered from blackouts? But Amber—what was wrong with Amber Snow?

Hilary watched her grandmother toss aside those strands of weedy white hair that rose and waved in drifting swells of heat.

She asked, "Where's Aunt Amber?"

Edythe yawned then, showing yellow dentures before her hand covered the withered cavity.

"Amber's not well, dear."

"Unless I was dreaming... I mean, she looked to me... misshapen. How sick is she?"

Edythe didn't answer.

"How long has she been like that?"

"Not too long," said Edythe.

"You've got me stumped, Grandma. How do you mean: not too long?" Hilary wasn't even sure she had her grandmother's attention.

"Well, what day is it?"

Hilary didn't know whether she was supposed to answer that or not. She'd been told in the past that her face was easily readable, a silent movie actor's face, and she didn't try to hide the confusion that she was sure must be there now.

"Oh, I'm sorry Hilary. I'm teasing you."

"Are you? You're confusing me."

"Believe me, Amber is just as healthy as she's always been."

"But her stomach?"

14

"Just an ailment. It's just a bloating. And now..." said Edythe as she rose from the chair. She moved to the sink. "*Now*," she said again as she swung her attention slowly back to her granddaughter with such calculated ease that Hilary never guessed that she was deliberately wasting time. As she passed the kitchen table:

"Have I told you how much I missed you?"

"Not yet this morning," said Hilary. Then, before she knew it, Edythe Snow was saying something about a few chores and was out the back door.

Hilary was hit by a cleaning bug; since the kitchen looked so good, why not the rest of the house. The floor needed sweeping badly. The rugs begged for a good shaking.

Sweeping, she found some interesting if not disturbing items.

Wadded behind the couch was what might have once been a dust rag, now it was encrusted with dried blood.

Under the couch was a partial animal skeleton—grisly however small it was.

And in the corners, entangled in dust and hair balls: things that could have once been living. Fury, bullet-sized mice perhaps, or beetles.

She didn't dwell much on any of these things, though. She didn't have time. She cleaned, true, but cleaning wasn't on her mind. All she could think was: was she alone in the house with Amber?

HILARY'S FATHER'S FUNERAL ENDED, leaving behind a feeling vaguely disquiet and a nimbus of dust that wouldn't settle. She felt bad that she had barely acknowledged those who'd attended Daniel Critchlow's funeral: Christian Snow and his uncle, Gloria VanCoth and the Benedict's who were Edythe's nearest neighbors, and her cousin Arizona Snow who lived in the village. Hilary went back to the Snow house. With her went the sun. The sky over Windsor piled up with clouds, a great white traffic jam. A faraway sound of thunder rolled down from them. Hilary went upstairs to her room, which never looked so wilted and so yellow, to get undressed, but for some reason getting undressed become quite a chore.

She lay down. There was a convoluted pattern on the ceiling she failed to notice before. She must have slept because when she looked at the travel clock she'd brought from home it was hours later.

She had no will to move. Edythe looked in, bringing her a cup of tea and toast. She found herself captivated by an old framed photograph over the bureau. Edythe's late husband, John Carlisle, sitting in a chair in his Oxford gray suit, was closely surrounded by an oval frame. In 1964, her grandmother had become Edythe Carlisle, but nobody had ever called her that; Edythe and Amber were, and would always be, the Snow sisters. The room grew dark but a darkness incomplete. It was a darkness speckled with static. Her clock ticked noisily.

She forced herself to rise. At the window she knelt, drinking in the fresh air. Over the top of the hill a full moon dangled precariously, bulging dangerously. As she watched, it convulsed and gave birth, spewing winged serpents, bats that slithered across Windsor's night sky. She forced herself to watch. Amber Snow was in the back yard, arms extended, screaming at the sky and at the laboring, emptying moon. The serpents flocked around her. Amber looked up at Hilary in the window and began to scream louder. Hilary's stomach began to ache.

She fell asleep, forgetting.

ALL SUNDAY SHE STAYED IN THE YELLOW ROOM, in bed, deep within blankets. She couldn't rouse herself for the burial. It rained unceasingly.

THREE

THE RAIN HAD STOPPED. Hilary took a bottle of Pepsi out on the porch and sat in the dark. There was a steady wind, carrying away the stale clouds and bringing in the fresh. The moon appeared every so often as if checking to see if she was still there. Hilary heard the mosquitoes moving along the porch ceiling but felt nothing. They weren't interested in her or else they hadn't found her yet. Rainwater dropping from leaves caused endless footfalls in the woods, it drizzled slow as oil off the porch roof into muddy puddles at the foot of the steps.

Edythe stepped out onto the sunken porch and sat down beside her.

"How is your cola," asked Edythe.

"Oh," said Hilary, taking a sip from the forgotten bottle. She burped inaudibly. "Um, bubbly."

"If you feel up to it, tomorrow would be the perfect day to explore the attic; it's going to rain all day again. There's old silver up there, and there's antique dolls. The silver I'd like brought downstairs."

"All right."

"Maybe you could help me clean it up, the silver, I mean. If you like it you can take it home with you. I can't possibly take it with me and I'd feel better knowing you have it. And look around up there for anything else you'd like to have."

The aspect was fundamentally depressing, Hilary said nothing.

Edythe looked up at a blue star that momentarily pierced the thin overcast. "It's going to be nasty tomorrow. You'll have enough to do to keep yourself busy inside."

"The moon," said Hilary, stretching. "It's beautiful. It's surrounded by a halo."

"That's Amber's moon."

Hilary was about to echo Edythe's last few words when she was interrupted by a disturbing noise from the woods. Scratchy. Desperate. If she were in a hospital she'd swear it was the wail, unmistakable as it was, of the just born. Coming from the woods it was horrific, terrifying—a perversion that an animal should sound so human. A deer leaped across the field in the dark, stopping once before it continued past the old foundation.

Worse than the cry from the woods was Edythe's reaction. She swooned on her thick-soled shoes, alerting the no longer preoccupied mosquitoes. By the light from the front room window Hilary could see that the strangled sound she made was bulging her neck.

"What's that?"

Edythe answered only with a garbled noise.

"Do you know?"

She backed slowly to the door. Frightened, Hilary moved with her. There was no bulb in the porch socket. They both pulled open the front door, and they both closed it behind them.

"These dreary woods," said Edythe wearily. She looked around her like an animal trapped. "Here in this old, decrepit house."

She climbed the staircase and sighed a good night. Then cast a warning down at Hilary who stood uncertain.

"Don't go outside."

SHE SWITCHED OFF ALL THE DOWNSTAIRS LIGHTS and stood in the dark at the window. Her half drank Pepsi was still out there. Hilary didn't have to imagine hard to see the fizz still rising to the darkly shinning surface. She watched for a while, ignoring the sweat that tickled her scalp, until her Aunt Amber appeared at the same place the deer had. She moved slowly, the moon had time to crawl across the sky as she fell to her knees a number of times.

Hilary bent close to the glass. Her nose touched it, she held her breath to keep it from fogging. Amber was closer—she collapsed again, spilling something into the grass. Now Hilary couldn't breathe.

When Amber picked up the tiny baby Hilary turned away, walked as though on tiptoe, like she balanced a book of tragedy on her head, straight and stiff as if she were moving in a trance. Her bed was a poor refuge. The sheets smelled of the house. Tell Edythe, she told herself, lying awake. Tell Edythe what you saw. Yet she realized she couldn't. She was too afraid that Amber would know she had seen.

FOUR

AMBER SNOW WAS NOT IN THE HOUSE, Edythe had searched for her everywhere. It was noon, and Hilary was in the attic, and although she couldn't hear the misty rain on the front porch roof that had been drifting down in sheets since she'd gotten up, Edythe could feel it in her bones. This could very well be her only chance and she had to act fast. Leaving the front door, she went upstairs, listening for Hilary's movements in the attic. When the rain came down harder, like an elemental warning, the newborn began to cry—yet Edythe did not let that hamper her cause.

Amber's bedroom was essentially bare. Amber's feather bed was so neat it looked unslept in, as Edythe stole passed it dust swirled up from the cotton blanket and pillow. There was nothing on the walnut dresser besides table linen and a bible.

The crying was coming from under the bed. Edythe bent down and dragged out a nest of blankets, then pulled back a folded corner and uncovered the little one.

She could not allow Amber another child.

The baby cried louder, turning scarlet. His fingers, puny, stubby things, shown like mother-of-pearl.

Slowly, her face bent so low she could feel the breath from the heaving little tempest, Edythe covered the child with the blankets loose corner. Her hand didn't leave the blanket, sure and steady it moved until she felt the button nose. Once she'd found the face her hand clamped down hard on it. Inside the house there was a sudden blessed silence. The maddening sound of rain leaped in. The child, trying to shake loose, managed to wiggle its naked behind.

In no time at all, the child was smothered.

AFTER THE CRYING STOPPED Hilary picked up the metal box and placed it on an old cherry divan. She fingered through the box, looking for anything that looked old. She pulled out a newspaper article.

Snow Sells Stock After Fire

Cortland Snow, whose house burned last week Wednesday, has sold his stock and his tenant, Mr. Carlisle has moved into a house across the river from Rt 79. He had an insurance of $1400 on the building and $400 on the contents in the Broome County Patrons' Fire Relief Association. All the family had left in clothing was what they had on. There were 75 bushels of potatoes in the cellar which was destroyed and about 100 cans of fruit, the later belonging to the Carlisle's.

Lightning caused the fire and was responsible for the destruction of the lightning rod of the house. The Windsor fire department responded to the alarm and was instrumental in saving a wood shed and poultry house near the house and the barn in which was the stock, hay, farming tools, etc.

"Damn rain," said Hilary. It made it difficult to read, it was so loud on the roof above her. She looked back in the box.

There was an old postcard with a black and white photograph of her father's store in Albany. Sept, 5 1978 it read. Hilary gathered a few more items together before making her way down the stairs. After closing the door behind her she crossed the room and entered an empty hallway. The sound of the rain wasn't so powerful and Hilary paused on the carpet, listening for it before starting down the second flight of stairs.

"Good morning," said a smiling Edythe, slicing cauliflower on a board next to the sink. There was very little light at the window. "Have you eaten lunch?"

"I haven't eaten breakfast." Hilary took her accustomed place at the table while Edythe poured her a cup of coffee. "Thanks."

"I'm making cauliflower soup for lunch," said Edythe in a voice that said this was, she believed, a special treat.

"Mmm," collaborated Hilary. "I love cauliflower soup." She sipped her coffee and unfolded the paper she brought down.

"Rain's letting up."

"I—heard a baby crying." Hilary watched as Edythe's expression remained still. "If it wasn't so crazy I'd think Aunt Amber had a baby last night."

"What baby? You might have heard an animal trapped in the attic. Under the floor boards, I bet."

"It was a baby," said Hilary.

"That's silly, dear. Amber's older than the hills."

"Well, I heard something. I guess I'm not sure what. Do you mind if I look around... just for my own peace of mind?"

"Might as well look now if you're going to look, before the soup is ready."

With her coffee steaming she searched every room on the second floor, starting with Amber's, sipping as she listened for even the slightest sound of a breath. The only sounds she heard were hers. In the sewing room, which contained the door to the attic, she came across a feather duster and began to dust as she looked. Almost an hour later, with an empty coffee cup and a much grayer feather duster, she re-entered the kitchen and sat at the table now set with soup bowls.

"Did you find the baby in question?" teased Edythe.

"I've looked everywhere but the cellar," answered Hilary seriously. When that broke into an embarrassed smile she covered her face with her hand, letting her blond hair fall over the table. She was lightheaded from hunger and the smell of the soup was intoxicating.

"Don't get upset, honey. You hear all sorts of things in the country." Pulling her sweater tighter around her, Edythe walked to the stove. She carried the huge pot of soup slowly, steadily back to the table where they ate soup every day for lunch for the next two weeks.

FIVE

HILARY RETURNED TO THE HOUSE from a trip to the Big M. Her grandmother's neighbor, Gloria VanCoth, was the cashier who rang her up and they'd talked for a short while. Hilary realized that there was no one home at the Snow house after she had put away the groceries. Edythe was not in her garden with those black rubber gloves that were huge on her. On her way out the kitchen door, Hilary considered that her Aunt Amber would some day die out here, in the woods, in the darkness under a tree. The thought disturbed her some as she headed out for a stroll. Maybe she'd find her grandmother, and the path behind the old foundation, now only a small depression in the ground, was as good as any. The three of them, the three Snow women (even though her last name was Critchlow, as Edythe's technically was), out on the land—it created a certain feeling in her. She imagined themselves as three shinning points of silver light, moving like a rotating triangle in the dark green lush.

The path was well beaten. It led her through tall grasses crowded with twisted, man-sized trees. The ground rose and Hilary was delighted to find the hill as she remembered it. Abruptly, the path turned out of the trees. She followed this for a short while.

Until she found the earthen mound.

It sat like a defunct throne in a small clearing. For some reason she was instantly fascinated, and she stood looking at it before she attempted to climb to the top. Behind it, the trees were dark with shadow, bringing the mound a spectacular clarity. It looked—and Hilary realized it was senseless—overwhelmingly real and overtly detailed.

And all this from the sunlight.

Then a cloudmass happened to hurry over. The trees behind swayed, the dead limbs knocking, uttering admonishment in their dry tongue. The cloudmass swelled and hurried away.

The mounds height, she noticed, was about the height of her bedroom window. When she climbed to the mounds summit she found she could see the second story of the house, the steep, chimneyed roof, and the window of her yellow room.

She sat down in the long grass to watch the cloudplay. To watch the light snatching forms out of the eroding forest; the shadows sucking them back in again. Summer's end was just around the corner and its departure would take the greater half of those shadows. Dark shadows replaced by pure, white snow. Hilary, surveying summer's end, wistful like she'd never been before, wanted suddenly to be here to see it. To watch, to forever watch, eager seasons, wax and wane.

"To watch," she said out loud, not bothering to look when two birds fled from the foot of the mound and into the shadows of the forest.

"From this very spot."

On meeting with the shadows the birds shot back out. They flew straight at her head as if to claw her eyes, disrupting a few strands of her blond hair. Unruffled, she smiled.

"The leaves in autumn."

Then she thought she saw her nephew Christian. He was moving in the woods where the birds had been, crossing from tree to tree. As soon as she'd saw him he was gone, hid by the shadows and their leaves.

"Christian," she called.

"Christian," came back from the shadows; not an echo, because it was too unlike her voice.

"Is that you, Christian?"

It wasn't; though the voice was like a child's voice, though stranger, watery yet thirsty still. What she saw next would be with her for always. The pitiless sun made the horror solid. She was not delirious—or was she? Feverish again, and dreaming?

A boy who was not a boy stood at the treeline. He breathed and blinked back the afternoon sunshine; his every movement verified that whatever it was, it was real. She saw a quivering in his thighs, the dark eyes roll as he surveyed the clearing.

He did not see her at first, but when he did the eyes sparkled and it may have been a smile that parted his lips. The transparent gums began to chew on a wormy little tongue which just protruded past new rows of teeth. The child raised its arms and ten stubby fingers wiggled with the anticipation of touch; like his tiny dribbling penis, they too looked boneless, tender as kelp.

An instinct nearly made her reach her arms out in a gesture if recipience.

He started toward Hilary and the mound. Something in the ground below her mumbled—a movement of soft earth.

The woods still held surprises. From that same spot where the birds had fled and this naked breach of nature emerged, now stood Edythe. Hilary stared at her, as fascinated by her as she'd been of the child. Edythe pointed what looked like a spear at the thing which looked to be a boy. Before Hilary could stop Edythe, by word or by action, Edythe pushed the spear forward. It caught the child just as he turned, puncturing his arm and tearing the flesh from it. Sunlight flashed on the liquid that flowed from the wound.

There was a brutal yowl and the child was gone.

"What is it?" Hilary yelled to the figure standing where the shadows and the bright clearing collided. Her heart thumped wild as an alarm. Everything suddenly became unreal except for herself—she felt as if she was behind a glass wall, dreaming so hard that the dream was about to break through the glass and bite her, waking her into a reality that was much worse than the dream.

"What is it?" she repeated and would have said it again and again until she got an answer if it hadn't been for the laughter from an unseen audience. More a mad cackle than a laugh; drawing both Hilary and Edythe's attention.

There was no surprise in seeing Amber Snow at the opposite edge of the earthen mound, leaning like a petrified tree stump, her white hair taken up by a modest stir of air into a Medusian array. Whatever was going on in her head wasn't apparent; her face was slack and barren. Only her eyes were as animated as her hair, for they moved from granddaughter to grandmother much like the reptile she was.

"He's our child," said Amber evangelistically clear. Her large stomach was gone. It was by far the worst shock. The dreamscape Hilary found herself in flexed to allow the improbability; the glass wall shattered. Below her, indisputable movement. And Amber's next words were just as sharp.

"He's your son. He's all of ours. Edythe is a killer."

Stunned into silence, Hilary turned toward the sound of a snapped branch too late. Edythe was gone, vanished as completely as the child monstrosity. When Amber began to climb the side of the mound toward where she sat, the tears came. Tears that she felt were justified. Amber Snow would soon, at any second, reach the mounds summit and somehow touch her, corrupting her with that contact. Hilary's figure would bloat just as Amber's had. She too would be recipient of the Snow family condition: a recluse, haunted by calamity. After all, who'd escaped it? Hilary's mother hadn't. A manic depressive, she'd been struck by insomnia until dying from lack of sleep. Now it was Hilary's turn for calamities touch. She could only wait, crying, her tears spilling onto the miniature hill.

CLUTCHED IN AMBER SNOW'S BLEMISHED HAND was an image carved from rotten wood. It was beyond Hilary's recognition. A vicious, embryonic dropping from some grim forest, perhaps; a creature fashioned out of the same earth from which Amber was made. Amber touched its teeth to one of Hilary's breasts.

Repulsed, Hilary shoved the thing away.

Amber squatted as if to relieve herself right there in the mounds center, but instead sunk her free hand into the grass and pulled up a large sod of roots and earth. Hilary stared down at the hole. Her tears came to an instant stop; the last one working its way downwards into the mound.

"My god," she whispered. Something in her belly wiggled. She had no feeling in her legs, they were attached to the hilltop.

She forced them to move and ran from the mound, falling once, seeing Amber lower herself into the mound, become swallowed by it, getting up and running again. Her thoughts took wing, beating her to her little yellow bedroom.

PART TWO:

Arizona Snow

FALL 1778

THE LAND REMEMBERS. There is more buried in the ground than bodies.

The Oneida village which spanned both sides of the river in the valley of the Susquehanna was known in their tongue as Ogehage. Over time and many different spellings it became known as Onaquaga, "Place of Hulled Corn Soup." Though mostly Oneida Indians, the Tuscaroran's moved into the valley in 1715 and created smaller settlements to the north and south. The Indian crossroads settlement became a fortified village and an outpost of the British Colonies. In 1735 Sir William Johnson, superintendent of Indian affairs, visited the village and instructed that a chapel be built to Christianize the Indians. Then in 1754 a fort had been constructed in the village, and Onaquaga became an important outpost. A mission was established there, along with other allies of the British. Onaquaga grew prosperous, with cattle and poultry, gardens and orchards of apple, pear, and peach trees. The people lived in comfortable, well-built squared log houses with stone chimneys and glass windows. Next to the church were a burial ground and a great stand of apple trees.

It was October 7th and the winter storehouses had just been filled when the son of an Indian trader, a young man whose name was Young Tyler, informed the Oneida Men's Council what he had been instructed to tell: In retaliation for joint British and Iroquois raids on frontier communities, the Continental Army led by Colonel Butler had been dispatched and would reach the valley and the village of Onaquaga by the next day.

The Council ordered that Onaquaga be abandoned. In a span of a day the people who lived and raised their family in the village packed what animals they could, their stocks, their food, their lives, and vanished into the forests. Council member Han Longtom and his six elders retreated to the place of council, hidden on the side of a hill overlooking the village and the valley, to wait and to watch.

Sitting quietly on the ground, the Council brought out fresh tobacco and a clean clay pipe. When the pipe came round to Longtom, he rose and addressed the elders respectively in their Indian names rather than the English names which they usually went by, beginning with Tho-wen-ga-ra-gwen (He who takes up the Snow Shoe) on his left, and closing with Te-wash-ko-te (The Standing Bridge) on his right. They waited. They ate corn soup and squirrel meat. Behind them was the ancient earthen mound they had both feared and worshiped. It was there when they arrived. It would be there when they were gone. The people of Onaquaga believed that long ago a fierce spirit had fallen into the mound from the moon. The face of this being was frozen in a wide-eyed, openmouthed grimace as if screaming in pain, and to look on it was instant death.

Colonel Butler and his soldiers arrived and took possession of the village at 11 o'clock at night. The Council watched from their hidden trail as Onaquaga was burned at sun rise. It was a great illumination; the end of everything, surely. They were watching when a band of soldiers moved into the woods. Longtom organized a watch; one on the trail, one on the hilltop. The rest of the elders went back to the place of council. They smoked and waited. A Clan Mother paced the trampled grass on top of the prehistoric mound where she had placed wampum, symbolic carved animals, and strings of shell beads.

Sehoy Green Wood's bare toe found a small hole.

HORSE SHOE JOE AND DAN'L BANOW came back from their watches without being summoned by Hon Longtom. That meant only one thing. The Council put out the pipe and stood. Banow told them the path was overrun with soldiers and Horse Shoe Joe said the same was true on the backside of the hill. Longtom and the Council understood that they were trapped.

The hole that Sehoy's toe found revealed a larger hole to her. When she made it wide enough, she dropped inside the mound. She climbed out. "Here!" she called to the others. "You can hide in here!"

They could hear the shouts of the Continental Army closing in around them. They could smell Onaquaga burning. They could taste it. The Council looked apprehensively in the dark hole.

"You have no choice," said Sehoy.

Longtom shook his head sternly. "No," he said. Fear burned in his large brown eyes. "I see something there. Darkness, that eats like an animal."

"You see only what you choose to see. I see a hiding place with room for everyone." The army was getting closer. "You have no choice," Sehoy repeated.

Horse Shoe Joe, Banow, Square Hooks, Hernt Elks, and Longtom climbed down in the belly of the earth. Sehoy and her husband Mashue, worried for their family, ran off into the forest before Longtom could stop them. No history book ever written would tell how they were captured. How they were tortured. How they were killed there on the hillside.

Yet the land remembers.

Sacrificial blood consecrates. Those who were slaughtered like offered animals permanently marked the land and scarred the character of the people who later came there. The forests of Windsor were filled with wandering revenants, cremated spirits of destroyed forests, slaughtered tribes, drowned valleys, ghosts of the lynched hanging from trees. The land not only remembers, it is impregnated with agonies.

ONE

GARY VANCOTH HAD BEEN LOCKED INSIDE a mute, motionless world for five out of his forty-five years. The brain-damaged policeman broke through that silence just once during the last half a decade; two years ago, for several fleeting hours, he emerged from his coma like state and thrilled his wife Gloria with unbridled conversation recalling his Ford truck and the names of his dogs.

In 2011, Gary was shot point-blank by a drunken man who was angry at the police for reprimanding him for bothering his neighbors. The officer had fallen into a coma. It was on the morning of July 11, 2014 that he stirred and started talking; for hours he talked. Then suddenly he returned to silence. The neurologist couldn't explain it. Gloria was encouraged; she continued to feed him from a children's spoon, changed his clothes, shaved him, sometimes she would set him in his favorite chair where he'd remain all day or sometimes days. But he didn't speak again. His doctor said that he was blind and for the past two years all she saw was the whites of his eyes.

Gary VanCoth didn't react to sound, to touch, or movement. He sat in the dark until she switched on a light. He ate when she fed him. Gloria yearned to hear his laughter again, but his voice was five years dead.

ARIZONA SNOW WAS DARK AND BEAUTIFUL with a temperament beautifully dark. There are strange pleasures in smooth and silky blackness, black satin, blackness shining. Shining, white on black. Arizona thought that the most sensual.

Arizona was a white woman, but her feather soft hair was raven black which cast a dark sheen down her tanned skin. Her eyes, black, were surrounded by long and lush black lashes beneath eyebrows like slashes of ink. On her arms, besides a few black moles, was a delicate shadowy swath of dark hairs. The clothes she chose to wear that day were deeper shades of a rural dusk, decorated with a copper broach and bracelets turned dark green.

On her breasts, a place only she would ever see, a liver colored birthmark that had first appeared a month ago was spreading upward. If this was unnatural she didn't know; she mentioned it to no one.

Her fingers moved over the sculpture she'd made out of polymer clay. The feline legs tucked under in a kneeling position not possible for the panther the sculpture represented. Its paws upon its breasts, breasts which were two deeply etched spirals with freshwater pearls at their centers. Triangular ears, pointed forward like horns. The eyes were sculpted large, with symbols—scalloped sun disks, wings, and crosses—encircling them. The panther's tongue licked its chops; Arizona had painted it pink.

Would this be the last one?

There were mirrors, many of them, in every one of her four rooms. She went to the nearest and did not have to pull down the collar of her blouse to see. The birthmark had moved to the base of her neck.

Yes, her last sculpture; Amber Snow had promised.

SHE COLLECTED HER SCULPTURES from various places around her small apartment and dropped them into a brown paper bag. A turtle, a striped bear, an owl, and a winged man. The kneeling panther went in last.

With the paper bag in hand, Arizona walked down the dimly lit apartment building stairs and stepped out onto Windsor's Main Street. There were a few people on the sidewalk, some staring at her as she walked past, her hand gripping the bag tightly. A worn out elderly couple outside the Subway showed her the decay that was to come. Peering in the art gallery window were twenty year old girls, her same age, wearing expensive clothes. Like polishing a turd, she thought. It was a hot September; heat rose from the sidewalk in front of her as though it were about to burn. Arizona kept her dark eyes straight ahead. She opened the gallery door and stepped in. Before leaving her apartment she had changed into a sack-like black dress that she tied tight around her waist with a red belt. Her heels clicked hollowly over the wood floor, sounding like there was a cavern beneath. Arizona walked around quickly to the empty display window. Setting the paper bag down, she looked at the girls outside. They hurried away. For no real reason, she lifted a sculpture from the bag and, making sure no body was watching her, set it down in the display window. Silently, except for the sound of her heels, Arizona slipped back out to the street.

Arizona had a tendency to overdress for everyday occasions like work at the liquor store, and underdress for important events (like the recent funeral for her uncle who'd owned a little bakery in Albany). Rather than get in her unair-conditioned car, she walked up Chapel Street in her heels and crossed the plaza parking lot. It was Saturday and Arizona could hear music playing in the bar at the far end of the plaza. The glass door of the Big M rolled noisily open; two women stepped out. Arizona, looking straight ahead, made a rapid stride past them but then she stopped. She turned.

Arizona's lower lip moved slowly.

"Do you know who I am?"

THE GROCERY DOOR WHOOSHED OPEN. It was just one step that Hilary saw, just a step and a turn of a heel and the young woman stopped.

A number of crazy things went through Hilary Critchlow's mind as she looked at her cousin. The afternoon sun obviously worried Arizona in some way. It revealed something weak about her, though for the life of her Hilary couldn't see precisely what. More incredible was the way she appeared to be pressing her legs together, grinding them, like a child having to take a terrible pee. Not surprisingly, she wore almost all black, a black so dark that Hilary wasn't able to tell if her clothing was one piece or two. Below her flat forehead the reflector sunglasses she wore suggested nihilism or a diffused violence in which Hilary could see herself as a tiny, insect-like figure on the grocery stores threshold.

"Yes," Hilary said. "You're Arizona Snow."

She could have said more. She could have asked much. But she didn't; she waited with the hope that her dark cousin would show a little of herself. In that moment she found that she didn't altogether dislike Arizona. Hilary herself held no mystery, at least she didn't think so. And there was an attractiveness in that quality.

"You're still in town? You told people at the funeral that you couldn't wait to get back to Albany."

Had she said that? Hilary couldn't remember.

"And your father's funeral was weeks ago." Arizona glanced at the other woman. She laughed. A guttural sound.

Hilary placed a hand on her companions arm. "Do you know Gloria VanCoth? She rents the house next door to Edythe and Amber."

Arizona paused. "Gloria, how lovely to see you again," she said icily.

"Bullshit," the woman said. Agitation clear on her face, she hefted her grocery bags and walked into the parking lot.

Hilary frowned at her cousin. She wasn't afraid of the girl, but Arizona seemed to walk on all levels at once. "Gloria just got me a part time job here at the Big M. I decided to stay in Windsor for a while. A little while, anyway." Hilary found herself staring at Arizona. Her lipstick was exactly the same color as the necklace she wore, as far as she could tell. The bright sunlight was fading from the sky so she wasn't sure if the discoloration on her upper chest was a burn scar or a birthmark. "I found a nice bed and breakfast on route 79," she added.

Arizona said nothing. She seemed to have finished speaking. She did a bad job at hiding a sneer behind her black hair which she had let drop before her shoulders and over her chest. As Hilary looked awkwardly at Arizona, her cousin slipped down the sidewalk and pulled open the liquor store door with a strange grace.

Hilary stood astonished and immobile, watching her go. Then she ran to catch up with Gloria.

AT NINE O'CLOCK Arizona set the liquor store alarm and locked the door. Once her apartment door was locked behind her she headed straight to the bathroom. She turned on the shower and got under its cold spray, her black dress and belt on the floor, her shoes and carnelian necklace on the toilet seat, and let the assault of the water take her.

Twenty minutes later Arizona stepped out of the shower and stood still a few minutes longer, wondering about her cousin Hilary, letting the water stream down her body in little droplets, each like a probing fingertip. The air felt warm after the frigid water. Even still, she was shaking.

After a glance in the mirror above the sink she forgot about her cousin.

Her breasts were tanless. They were a liver-red where they should have been white. Her neck was dark yet the mark extended onto it, discoloring her tan as if with a stain of blood.

It was not blood. That washes off.

Since morning the mark had spread into and beyond the hollow of her throat. It was moving faster.

She could barely stand to look at herself. It was not right that she should go through this. She was promised that this would be stopped.

She had made the sculptures.

She was dark and so beautiful.

She stared at the mark on her neck. She bent closer.

Was that a flaw she detected in the mirror, an imperfection in the glass that threw her reflection off? There had to be. Either that or the mark had just climbed higher right before her eyes.

TWO

I T WAS DARK WHERE HILARY WAS. There was no real dream; no
state of subconsciousness whatsoever. Yet she wasn't alone.

She woke, exhausted.

It was a sunrise surrounded by golden cumuli. Ten minutes later
the sky left no doubt that it would be another irresistible day. But it
was a promise broken. By noon the sky was thick with dark clouds
and rain and it was as if the sun never was.

The view from her Barn Side Suite window was much the same
as the view from her little yellow room. A proud mound of deep
green rising over the river valley to nearly the center of the murky sky.
Rain speckled the window Hilary sat at and the last rays of the
extinguished sunlight shown a weird scheme across her face. Not far
away the television droned on but its back was to her, its theatrics
wasted on an empty love seat and an amateurish painting entitled,
inanely, Elm Pond Mallards. The paneled walls and ceiling glowered
dully in the lamplight and knotholes peered darkly at her from every
side like black eyes. Sure enough, someone knocked on her door as
she finally set herself to the task of calling Edythe.

It had been one month yesterday that she'd left the Snow house.
In a near-trance she'd found a place to stay and sat in it all that
evening and all night. Finally at the break of day she'd fallen into a

hollow sleep where she didn't exist anymore, she was a consciousless part of darkness. No loss would have been felt if she never woke up.

The knock on the door was tentative. Gloria was probably concerned that she might have been overly intrusive when she planned Hilary's day; but she wasn't. Hilary was expecting her. Her new friend wanted to drive the two of them to downtown Binghamton for a morning of shopping and then lunch was at Gloria's house. The house next door to Hilary's grandmother. The friendship turned out to be a convenient arrangement. Hilary had remained in Windsor to watch Edythe and Amber, now she could do that at arm's length.

"Just a second!" she called as she made a stop in front of a mirror. Seeing that there was nothing to fix added to her confidence.

The shopping excursion turned out a disappointment, though she did manage to find a pair of shoes for work comfortable enough to stand in. The rain did stop but the sky remained dark. It was two o'clock when they got back and the car headlights were on as they drove up the dirt road. There were only two houses on this road, the Snow house and the house Gloria rented from Hilary's grandmother. There was a low mist forming on the road. A few minutes later they pulled into Gloria's driveway.

The front of the house had a pergola which supported an unwieldy trumpet vine. Hilary paused to smell one of the large orange blooms. "No smell," she said. "No smell," echoed Gloria. "Just a mess when they decide to drop off." Inside, the house was filled with comfortable furniture and the smell of nutmeg with an underlying hint of coffee. Gloria asked Hilary if she would stuff the tomatoes which were already prepared, while she checked on her invalid husband. The stuffing was cream cheese, chopped stuffed olives and tomato pulp moistened with French dressing and mustard. Two dishes had been left out on the countertop. Hilary had the tomatoes served on salad greens, and then found Gloria in a small room off the living room, what in the old days they called a sewing room. There were flowers on a side table, and a small bookcase filled with washcloths, towels, tissue boxes, cotton balls, and rubbing alcohol. Next to the bed was what looked like a trapeze. Gloria's husband sat in a chair. His clothes were ill-fitted. His hands were in his lap. There were large bandages on his forehead and on the left side of his temple; he faced straight ahead yet his eyes were sightless, they were white, they were bloodshot.

Gloria saw her. "Come in," she said.

Hilary stepped in the room. Gloria had told her some of what had happened five years ago. "Can… can your husband hear us?" she asked quietly.

Gloria shook her head. "I don't know. Gary has no response to his surroundings, to voices or touch. He breathes, and sometimes I can stand him up. When I feed him he swallows." She shrugged. "I talk to him but, I don't know, sometimes I…"

Hilary smiled sadly. "Hello Gary," she said. "My name is Hilary. I'm your neighbor's granddaughter."

The ex-police officer sat motionless; the clock on the wall ticked loudly, too loud. A chill ran down Hilary's spine.

"The bandages on his face? Is he…" Hilary paused.

"They're just to cover the scars," Gloria told her. Then she whispered: "I couldn't stand to look at them any longer."

ARIZONA WAS WAITING on Edythe and Amber Snow's porch when she saw her grandmother come out of the woods. She met Amber at the corner of the house, on the houses wild side, weedy and neglected. Amber's face was dirty, her hands black with filth. Arizona held one of her carvings, the kneeling panther with the pink tongue.

"I thought if I made these the mark would stay away. I thought that's what you told me."

Amber made a noise like a wild cat.

"I thought I wouldn't have to go into the mound again."

Amber muttered an indiscernible sentence, though when she wanted to she could speak clearly enough.

"What do I do now?"

Amber smiled toothlessly. "Take them," she said.

Arizona looked away from Amber's midsection and asked, "Into the mound?"

Amber licked her lips with a blackish tongue. "Take them. Yes. Gifts for the dead."

ARIZONA SNOW REVISITED THE ANCIENT MOUND standing proudly in the woods behind the house. For the first time she noticed how the trees circling the clearing were slowly pressing in. The forest was compressing the clearing smaller and smaller. For the first time in her score of years she paused to ponder time. Some day the groveling forest would reach the sanctified feet of the earthen mound. She remembered going into the mound. Once. She couldn't remember how long ago. She remembered it had been night. And that a multitude of bats came down from the starlit treetops to greet her like a cult of screaming woman. But that was all she remembered.

From the mounds grassy top, a little more than a story high, she slipped off her clothes and let them fall where they may. In the grass they looked like dark holes.

The mark on her skin, amoebic looking, covered half her front torso. It enclosed her breasts like a lover's hands, unwilling to be removed. A shapeless member reached toward her abdomen, another brushed her lips with a purple, bloated finger.

Below her, within the mound, was darkness, yes, but more than that. Mystery lay within it. Mystery too deep, deeper than darkness.

"Imagine the grass, hair."

She grabbed a handful, lifted it.

"Imagine the sod, a head."

Dark soil hung from the sods dangling roots. It *was* head shaped, though too large. The roots were like stringy veins. The bits of falling soil like black blood dripping from the stringy veins.

Arizona stared down into the real hole among the holes that were her dark clothes. There, in the hole, the darkness; *see it?*

"I can't feel the darkness but it can feel me."

THE HILLS OF WINDSOR

She talked to the thing in the darkness. She stepped in and sat on the edge. The grass played in her ass. Her feet swung in the hole. She talked as if to a lover.

"I can't touch the darkness... but it can touch me."

Strong hands on her legs, strong muscles around her calves: yet there was nothing. She slid her hips over and down, arms locked straight, grass crushed beneath her palms.

It played with her. The darkness barged reckless between her thighs.

Lower. Lower.

She sank, arms bending. The long grass tickled her nose then she smelled the musky maleness of earth. Simultaneously, her pupils widened, she left the afternoon light.

Her breasts jostled: they wagged supernaturally as if licked by a giant tongue. Lapping at the mark on her skin as if it was the residue of red wine.

Exhilarated, Arizona pulled the sod back into place and dropped into mystery.

IT WAS A SUNNY, BREEZY MONDAY MORNING and Gloria VanCoth had a mystery at hand. As it happened, today was Hilary's first day at work while it was Gloria's day off. She'd hung up wash in the early morning and had just now noticed that some of her husband's clothing was missing from the clothes line. Of course it was possible wind could have blown them off. She searched her back yard but failed to find anything. She tapped her finger on her lower lip when she found a couple broken clothespins. Gloria tried to remember exactly what items she had hung up.

Standing with her hands on her hips in her yard, she couldn't see the Snow house but she could see the small depression in the ground that once served as the cellar for the Snow family's original house. That house was long gone and the cellar had gradually become filled until only a weed-covered hollow remained. Gloria thought she saw a flannel shirt down in the depression. She walked across the yard and started down, wading through knee high grass. It was a slight decent. And it wasn't a flannel shirt. It was a dark blue pair of pants.

Gloria picked the pants up off the ground and snapped them in the breeze. She looked around. Two steps away was an unusual piece of wood lying on top of trampled grass. She picked it up.

It was an Indian. Crudely yet exquisitely carved out of wood. It looked very old. The Indian was the size of her hand, and plump, like a fertility idol or a fetish. It sat comfortably in the hollow of her palm. Gloria made a puzzled face at it: Where did it come from? It reminded her of the Zuni animal carvings Gary had bought in New Mexico the year before the shooting.

Gloria made one more quick search for the missing clothes, and then took the little wooden Indian inside.

THREE

IT WAS MONDAY EVENING. The night of the full moon. It appeared over the lonesome pines a titanic, larger than life. The moon's shadows, mountain shadows, were of the same pale blue as the surrounding sky, giving the full moon not the appearance of the real moon but of a ghostly sister. As she moved above the horizon she shrank to a wizened figure of the former giant. Doing so, she grew strong—separating from the darkening blue sky.

Never before had it been so close, Edythe Snow thought as she stared at the moon. She should have expected it today. They were an old cycle, her and her sister. Were they expected to live forever? Edythe felt too old; she was old. Perhaps that was why her sister's attempts at murder were getting more frequent and more deadly serious.

Edythe was thankful her granddaughter wasn't here to see it. Hilary had been finishing up her first day at work when it happened. Edythe was outside sweeping the front porch. As she was doing so, Amber had burst out of the heavy front door wielding a kitchen knife above her extended belly as if it were a plump pumpkin about to be cut. She came at Edythe. Edythe used her broom to defend herself.

Amber savagely threw the knife. It turned in the air, hitting Edythe broadside in the throat. Then she watched as her sister toddled away, carrying that monstrously enlarged stomach into the woods.

Now, staring vacantly at the full moon, the first real autumn breeze suddenly made the sixty-five degrees feel very chilly. Edythe rubbed her neck and wondered about what would be born this night.

HILARY WAS ALARMED at the bruise on her grandmother's neck but Edythe would hear none of it. From the kitchen table, she watched Edythe rinse tea cups in the sink. Hilary got up from the chair and came up behind the old woman and pulled out twigs which were caught in her hair.

"How do you feel, Grandma?" she asked.

Edythe started to speak, started to do something, and stopped. She said, "I'm alive."

Hilary touched Edythe's temple, could feel the veins there. Her forehead was cool.

There was something she wanted to ask. Something straining to be—

"What..."

To go back to the spinning vortex.

"... did you... do... with Aunt Amber?"

The question was ludicrous. Why had she asked it?

Both women looked up when they heard a car door slam shut outside. Hilary walked past her shoes in the hall and, barefoot, pushed open the front door. She stepped out into a cool morning shadow, stepped again into radiant sunshine like a hot towel on her feet. Arizona had just straightened after rearranging suitcases behind the driver's seat. Hilary looked at her cousin; it was Arizona who now turned to face the porch, but an Arizona transformed. Her darkly tanned skin was as clear as a September night in Windsor. Shining darkly, her hair drew in the sun rays and sent up heat waves in the air. Her eyes held Hilary like mirrored moons, with her eyes within the moons. She wore a jet black skirt and wrap-around top. Hanging low on her neck was a sting of carnelian beads.

"Suitcases? Where are you off to?" asked Hilary.

"South," Arizona said simply.

"Um."

"I'm getting on route 11. It will take me straight to New Orleans."

Hilary was slightly disturbed by the look in Arizona's eyes. As she watched the look got harder.

"I'm getting as far away from here as I can get. I'm going to start a new life. I'm owed that."

"I may not be here when you get back," Hilary told her. "So, it was nice to see you."

Arizona's eyes softened to a liquid darkness.

"Hilary, where is the man in your life? Why are you here, were you forced?"

"*Forced.*" Hilary laughed, nervously. "Of course I wasn't forced."

"But no man to hold you back?"

Now she felt forced. Arizona was pressuring her to confess to the dismal facts of her life. She wasn't going to give her cousin the satisfaction.

"I have a wonderful relationship up in Albany," she lied, making clear her annoyance. "He's waiting for me."

Arizona looked doubtful.

THE NIGHT WAS UNEXPECTEDLY WARM. Yet a warm night was not always good. Tonight it was not. The moist earth and air turned the heat sour, making it a night for insects.

She found one of Amber's children in Wishwa Glen, where one or two always ended up, stumbling or slithering over the loose stones of the creek. Edythe walked toward it.

The baby at her feet lay in the splashing water, absorbing it, and becoming hideously bloated. It became aware of her presence; it shuddered, it rolled over onto its side.

It waited, somehow knowing: death by impalement; yet still it swallowed water, and faster. Hardly amazed, Edythe watched it grow larger, its sides ballooning.

Death by impalement. Edythe lifted the spear. The eighty-five year old muscles in her arms gathered into tight balls. She hesitated, staring when more of it was reveled to her as clouds parted before the moon. It writhed as if already feeling the killing blow. A mouth, swelling lips, gleamed in the moonlight as, never pausing, it drank and drank and drank.

Upon impalement the baby exploded. Warm water splashed on Edythe. She washed, kneeling in creekwater.

One down.

Not so bad, she thought. Of course there was a time, not so long ago, when she could get them all. Now she was tired. She turned and headed home.

SOMETHING WAS WRONG. Gloria felt it first in her garden. Moles had devoured half of her cucumbers, but it wasn't that. Later, outside sorting recyclables in the garage, she felt it again. A feeling of being watched. It was warmer than usual for September. Humidity knocked on the garage windows, determined to get in. She drove to work.

"Have you heard?" a co-worker asked her as she passed in a hurry to the grocery stores back room.

About the heat? Gloria thought. How could she not have noticed?

"Of course you haven't!" said Maxine Meister, unable to slow her speech down. Apparently, she was also unable to stand still. "They didn't find him that long ago. Now..." and here Maxine's voice became veiled, her hand guarded the right side of her lips as if she was trying to cup the words inside it, so she could discreetly discard the spillage later. "Now, my boyfriend is a cop, Hilary. He told me the police found Joe Harmer in the field behind his house. He was dead. Dead and messed up. Doesn't he live somewhere near you?"

"What do you mean? Messed up."

"My boyfriend said his neck was broken. So were both his arms."

At four o'clock Gloria left work. She backtracked home, parked her car in the driveway, and got out. And then she saw him, a man standing in the woods. She couldn't see his face but otherwise he was in plain sight. He was wearing a familiar shirt. L.L. Bean. Scotch plaid red and green. It was the birthday shirt she had bought Gary. It was a shirt missing from her clothesline.

Gloria ran in the house. The door to her husband's bedroom was closed. She always left it open.

She looked in. Gary was sitting upright in his chair. The curtains were closed and it was near dark in the room. His face was eradicated, featureless. "I'm home, Gary" she said.

Gloria crept back to the front door and looked outside. There was no one in the woods. And still...

the feeling

...that something was terribly wrong.

AND SO IT WAS FOR EDYTHE SNOW as she walked through the woods. The old woman had spied him a number of times, a slim, pale, milky thing that had grown quickly to half the size of a man. How many others could have reached adulthood? Surely no more than a few. The old woman wandered, cursing here and there at a rogue tree branch or a lichen covered rock. She listened. Not only for the cry of babies but for Amber. Although death did not sound altogether unattractive to her right now, she wasn't going to let her sister be her executioner.

Head cocked, she followed her instincts. Climbing over the trunk of a fallen tree, she looked down for just a moment. When she looked up again the child was there. He looked back at her over the smooth ball of his shoulder, his cow-like eyes slowly oozing clear liquid.

Whatever he was doing he stopped. Edythe began to sing softly. It wasn't necessary, but it struck her fancy. This was an older child. This might be her last chance.

"Rock-a-bye baby..."

The wind rustled in the branches.

"In the tree top..."

Edythe took a few cautious steps forward.

"When the wind blows...

the cradle will rock."

49

Her song was just above a whisper. Filtered daylight flickered under the swaying trees. The child stared at her as though the words meant something to him.

"When the bough breaks… the cradle will fall."

Her steps came quicker. Now she was rushing forward.

"And *down* will come *baby*…"

The spear, rising high.

"… *cradle*

and

all."

Her song had gained force as with her intent, rising to a shrill cry of success. She was just about to push the spear home when, the instant before, Amber stepped through the shafts of daylight with an old shotgun raised in her veiny hands. The gun was once Edythe's husbands, unfired since his death in 1964.

The shot was not unlike a bolt of lightning. Edythe stood unhurt and shocked, her ears ringing, staring at the shotgun which was now a smoking mess of twisted metal. As it dropped from Amber's hands Edythe saw that one of her sister's fingers was missing.

Yet Amber didn't seem to notice. With a bloody hand she shooed away her offspring. Edythe quickly moved to strike again, but it was too late. The child had disappeared into the woods.

SHE COULD HAVE KILLED HER SISTER. She had the spear. Something stayed her, though, some moral principle she could not break. But she'd come so close, standing face to face with Amber, her spear between them, its point at Amber's pendulous belly—

Edythe remembered a day in the life of a little girl:

It had been Halloween. Amber Snow, not yet ten, held a spear—then a mere fishing spear—at Edythe menacingly, as if intending to stab her there in the shed. This spear, Edythe now recalled, her sister had used to find the entrance to the mound. It was the first object to pierce the dark cavity within.

As soon as the thought appeared it fled; but it was enough, thank goodness, and like the memory her chance at damnation was gone. Amber ran like a crooked witch into the woods.

Edythe shook with rage as she turned toward the house. She wished she had Hilary to go home to. There would be some small comfort, meager as it was, in performing the daily rituals for her granddaughter's benefit. Now the array of charades was over.

Edythe returned to a quiet house, a house of empty whispers. She changed her clothes, half expecting Amber with a hatchet in her hand. She slipped her slippers on. She made toast and tea, unconcerned. A rain, gentle as a corpses touch, ran along the roof and down the chimney, tapping in the fireplace. No, Amber would not be home tonight.

FOUR

HILARY SET HER COFFEE CUP ON THE TABLE and stood by the window looking out at Gloria's back yard. It was 2:35 in the afternoon. They had the same hours at the Big M and the plan was to go in together. Hilary hadn't taken the part-time job at the supermarket out of necessity, she wanted to do it. It was better than sitting alone all day in her suite, staring at the Elm Pond Mallards.

"It looks like it's going to be an early fall," she said with a raised voice. "The trees are changing already."

She heard Gloria say something back.

"We have to be at work in less than half an hour," Hilary said louder. "Are you almost ready?"

Hilary looked for her in the small room off the living room. Gloria was washing her husband's face with a washcloth. "I'm almost ready," she told Hilary. She leaned close to Gary's ear. "It's my friend Hilary. She's here to take me to work, isn't that nice?"

Hilary could hear him breathing. He sat as rigid as a board. His eyes showed only bloodshot white. Gloria picked up a partially eaten bowl of tomato soup and a plastic spoon. Then she pointed to the side table. The flowers were gone and a wooden Indian stood in their place.

"That's the carving I found out back."

Hilary picked it up. She shook her head. "Strange," she said. "It looks pretty old."

"Yes. That's what I thought," said Gloria as she folded some clothes. "Have you talked to your grandmother lately?"

"Yesterday."

"How is she doing?"

Hilary smiled. "The same as always." She shrugged. "My cousin Arizona left town last week."

"I saw her next door at your grandmother's house," said Gloria. "Oh, about a week before your father's funeral. I told her that she looked nice."

"What did she say?"

"She told me to drop dead."

Gloria's comatose husband blinked.

Hilary's laugh turned into a gasp.

"What's the matter?" asked Gloria.

Hilary pointed. "Your husband just blinked his eyes."

Gloria turned toward Gary. She looked at his face closely. "That happens, sometimes."

After Gloria put up her hair and they were walking over the gravel driveway to Hilary's car, Gloria looked thoughtfully at her friend.

"Can I ask you something personal? About your family, I mean."

For a second there was uncertainty in Hilary's eyes. "Sure," she said. "Anything."

"How exactly is Arizona related to you? Is Edythe her grandmother?"

"No. My Aunt Amber is her grandmother."

"Amber? I haven't seen her in… ages. How is she doing?"

Hilary didn't answer the question. Instead she said: "Both Edythe and Amber had a child out of wedlock in the late 40's. Amber had Alvin, and a year later Edythe had Edmund. Arizona is Alvin's daughter; he was older, like fifty, when she was born. I have no idea who the mother is; I don't think Edythe or Amber know, either. Then my grandmother got married in 1960 and my mom was born."

"And you told me that your mom died when you were two."

"Yes. Then Aunt Amber married sometime after Alvin was born and her husband died a year later."

"Wow. I see. And your nephew Christian is Edmund's son's child. Edythe is his great-grandmother. He stops in the Big M a lot. By the way, Swedish Fish is his candy of preference."

Gloria thought that Hilary looked uncomfortable. "I'm asking too many questions, aren't I?"

"Don't be silly, of course not."

"All right, one more question. So, there's only three Snow's left: Arizona, Christian, and you. I mean, besides your grandmother and aunt."

"My mother went by the name Snow. My last name is Critchlow."

"I know,' said Gloria. She raised her eyebrows at Hilary and smiled a little mischievously. "But, Edythe and Amber are getting pretty old. Who's going to inherit the house and liven the place up with little ones?"

"Little ones?"

"Babies, I mean."

Hilary almost looked ill, but then she smiled faintly. "Christian is only thirteen. He's got plenty of time. We better get going or we'll be late."

The sound of a roaring engine stopped them from getting into Hilary's car. Both women turned toward the road to see a car hurtle past in a cloud of dust. Hilary cocked her eye at Gloria. "Arizona's back."

"She seems in a hurry."

"Well, we have to leave now, but when we get back I'll go next door and find out what she's up to."

Working at the supermarket was a welcome distraction, and though she'd rather be working with her father in his shop in Albany, Hilary was getting to know the people of Windsor through the Big M. Henry Jeffers, the pastor at one of the Methodist churches, invited her to Sunday service. His wife asked if Hilary would like to join her at a local quilt show. Ann Dressel, a local yoga instructor, offered her a yoga mat for Yoga in the Park in the nearby Klumpp Park. And at the end of the day, with a flushed face, farmer Max Tingley informed her and all within earshot that there was another body found this morning, this time on the Village Green.

The supermarket closed at 9:00 and Hilary drove Gloria straight to her house. It was dark. Snow land was very quiet. The gravel crunched under Gloria's feet as she made her way around the car. Hilary rolled down her window.

"Are you going to stop back," Gloria asked, worried. "Just so I won't be wondering all night."

Hilary nodded her head. "I'll be back. If Arizona had some sort of emergency, I'm sure my grandmother would have called me. I think she would."

"I'll wait then."

"You should wait inside."

"I will. Be careful, Hilary."

There was a silent moment between them; intuition needed no explanation.

"I'll be back soon."

Gloria entered the house and walked through the empty rooms, picking up a newspaper here and an empty coffee cup there. In Gary's room, it was dark but everything looked neat and tidy. She stood by her husband's chair and turned on the lamp which had always had a touchy switch. She turned it too far, and the light switched on and winked out, but in that second she saw his face: Gary's mouth was open in a silent scream, his blind eyes wide beneath hairy eyebrows. A second later and she had the light on again. Gary's face was glacial; indifferent; Gloria shuddered, unfriendly even.

"Hi, honey," she said to the room. "I'm home from work."

She knelt in front of him with tears in her eyes. "How was your day?" she said sadly.

Then she noticed Gary had the little Indian in his lap.

HILARY PUSHED OPEN THE HEAVY DOOR without knocking. Her grandmother's house seemed as quiet as Gloria's, but there was sound to be heard if she stopped to listen. Branches did break in the woods when she had crossed the yard. If nothing else, the air moved in there.

She walked around the front room, looking at the old, dusty furniture and the wooden banister curled like a big brown snake, suspending itself above the staircase leading up to the usual darkness. She crossed the dining room rug and walked through the kitchen, then down a short hall to find herself at the staircase again.

For a few minutes Hilary stood at the bottom of the steps, gazing up at the darkness. Then she slowly moved up them. Her eyes were adjusting; she could see light seeping out into the hallway from under the spare bedroom door. She opened it and looked in. Black clothes on the bed; Arizona's suitcases on the floor. She continued down the hallway and heard noise in the bathroom. Someone was taking a shower. The next door was her grandmother's. She started to try the doorknob and her forearm brushed against... it felt like a rope. She pushed the door with her shoulder. It wouldn't budge.

The rope was tied around Edythe's bedroom doorknob and stretched taunt across the hallway to Amber's door, where it was also tied. Neither woman would have been able to open their doors from the inside.

"Grandma?" she said, slightly hoarse. She waited and then a weak voice:

"Who is it?"

"It's Hilary."

Louder: "Help me! Let me out!"

A light came on inside the bedroom, spilling out under Edythe's door, and it took many minutes to untie the knot in the semi-dark. When she finally had it, Hilary pushed open her grandmother's door. Edythe was standing near the light switch on shaky legs. Her face was dirty. The top of her dress was ripped and the buttons were missing.

"Am I alive?" asked the old woman.

"Yes, you're all right," Hilary told her, hoping it was true. "What happened? Who locked you in your room?"

Edythe appeared to be reassured by Hilary's presence. Her shaking stopped. Her panic vanished. Hilary tried to sit her down on her bed; Edythe would have none of it.

"Let's go downstairs, dear," she said to Hilary in a soft voice.

"Grandma, I think you should pack some things and come home with me. To Albany, I mean. I think you should get away from here."

"It's not as bad as that. I have everything I need here. Is it raining?"

"Not at the moment. Why?"

"I need to wash my hands. Let's go downstairs."

Edythe calmly walked out of her bedroom. Hilary stood open-mouthed, watching her go, then followed her into the hall. She touched the old woman's arm. Someone was climbing the stairs. The light spilling into the hall from Edythe's bedroom showed Hilary the one thing she did not want to see. It was Amber. Her hair a massive shock of white. She looked horribly old. And the housedress she wore was stretched to the ripping point over her swollen abdomen.

She held a hammer over her head as she crept up the last step.

When she saw Hilary, she treated her great-niece to a toothless smile.

The ghastly smile didn't last long. Suddenly more light spilled into the hallway. The bathroom door had swung open and Arizona, wet and naked, stepped out. Hilary turned and stared. Arizona's breasts jutted outward above a glistening, hugely distended stomach. She looked pregnant, but Hilary had just seen her the week before.

Arizona took five swift strides and she was on Amber Snow. Hilary had never seen such a look of shock on a ninety-year-old person's face. Amber swung the hammer and missed Arizona's head by less than an inch. The struggle lasted for only a moment. Arizona separated herself and both women stood in identical, terrifying silhouette. Then Arizona violently shoved Amber backwards down the stairs. The sound of her tumbling body was amplified under the low ceiling.

Arizona immediately ran down and stood over the prone body. She hissed unidentifiable words, than ran naked and pregnant through the door Hilary had left open and disappeared into the night.

Hilary stepped in front of her grandmother and looked down the stairs. Amber's water had broke. It seeped out on the dark wood floor from between her crooked legs. As Hilary watch from what felt like a thousand miles away, something moved under Amber's blue housedress. Something began to crawl out.

Hilary knees began to buckle. Then everything went black.

SHE WOKE UP IN A DAZE, not knowing where she was. It was night and the stars were out. She was lying in tall grass. Dark shadows moving around her were treetops. She felt high on a dais in the midst of the trees.

She knew exactly where she was. She sat up and realized that from her knees down her legs were dangling in a hole. She screamed. In one spasm of movement she pulled her legs out and turned to crawl away. A hand grasped her ankle, digging into her bone. She closed her eyes and screamed again. Not too far away a newborn began to cry. The hand let go.

Hilary stood up and ran. She didn't stop until she was locked in her car. She didn't stop crying until she was in Gloria's arms. And she didn't go back to the Snow house again. Not that year. Two days later she was 140 miles away in Albany.

For Hilary it wasn't far enough.

FIVE

WINDSOR WAS UNDER A SPELL the rest of the summer and through the fall. Gloria swore she could feel a chill over the village after a family mysteriously vanished, leaving behind a blood-stained room. John Thomas from Long Island, his wife Elaine, and their children, Michelle and Mitchell, vanished from their vacation home on the river. The neighboring cottage called police after the family's swimming pool overflowed. The police found the house locked, the burglar alarm turned off and no indications that any valuables had been stolen. But fresh bloodstains were found in John and Elaine's bedroom. It was the only conversation Gloria overheard in the store isles. And then when the family was found in a nearby cornfield, apparently murdered senselessly, a final hush fell over the river valley.

Conversations became guarded, and were kept at home.

"My friend Hilary sent us a lovely card. You remember Hilary, don't you? She moved back home to Albany."

Gloria sat on her husband's perfectly made bed. The clock ticked loudly. She gazed at the little wooden Indian and sipped her pumpkin-spice flavored coffee. It fell over. She leaned forward and placed it on its feet again.

"I suppose I could look downstairs for some sandpaper and sand him flat." She looked at her husband. "He doesn't like to stand up."

Gary sat as if transfixed.

"I have Hilary's e-mail address. I promised her I'd keep my eye on her nephew." She took another slow sip of coffee. "With all the deaths and disappearances in town, he hasn't been coming into to the Big M, which is a good thing, but I think I'll stop by his house. Do you remember the little boy Christian? He was seven when his parents were found under the Bridge Street bridge. That was right before you went into the hospital."

The doorbell rang. Gloria sighed and got to her feet.

There was no one there, of course. The porch was empty. So was the driveway. A bird screeched at her from the woods. Gloria went back to her husband's room. Gary was sitting at attention. It wasn't the first time she noted that his wide lips were set in a way that could almost be a smirk. The clock on the wall that Gloria had begun to hate must have just stopped ticking.

The Indian was fallen over. She set it back up.

"Windsor is under a spell," said Gloria again.

PART THREE:
Christian Snow

WINTER 1655

O N DECEMBER'S LAST DAY, William Lovel was working late selling the New Year's cookies that had carried his fame far down the Hudson River from his bakery in Beverwyck, a town that would be under English control within ten years and renamed Albany, after one of the titles of James, the Duke of York, brother to King Charles II. As trade slowed down, the baker took an extra horn of rum and was about to close up shop when an uncommonly tall and angular man wearing a fashionable beaver hat thrust his way in, demanding a dozen of the special cookies bearing an effigy of Saint Nick.

When the baker handed him the fragrant bag, the stranger said crossly, "One more cookie, I said a dozen."

"You have a dozen," said Lovel. "I counted them myself. Twelve of my New Year's cookies."

"One more cookie," said the tall man, muffled in a black cloak. "One more than twelve makes a dozen."

Lovel grabbed the man by his cloak and tried to push him to the door. "You can go to the Devil for another cookie!" Lovel shouted. "You won't get it here."

The stranger made no move to go. He turned and Lovel saw a round white face as featureless as unbaked dough.

"You have three lovely daughters."

"Who is telling you this?" demanded the baker.

"Red-lipped maidens, just on the verge of girlhood."

William Lovel retreated behind the polished wood counter, where he placed his hand on his musket. The stranger opened the bakery door and a fiercely cold gale wind blew in.

"Close the door, sir!"

The lanterns flickered out, one by one.

"Close the door, sir!"

It was imposable, that all the lanterns would go out as they did. Lovel snatched his musket from under the counter. He leveled it instantly. Leveled it in the dark. In the glacial cold. A voice boomed out: "One of those lovely maidens has met a young man! Off a ship from England! A young man named Snow!" A cold, bony hand grasped Lovel's wrist and the musket fell from his hands. And then a whisper, close to his ear: "I wanted to be here at the beginning, as well as at the end."

Suddenly the lanterns were lit. William Lovel was alone in his bakery. On the floor lay a spilled bag of his famous cookies.

Lovel tried to quell his shaking with great gulps of rum. He grabbed his musket and a lantern and was out the door, into the snow. Something on the frozen path caught his eye and he bent down. It was a human footstep painted in the snow, painted in blood.

Following the footsteps passed the Dutch style gabled hotel one door down, then up the dirt street through a cluster of wagons, Lovel reached a rock beetling over the river shore. There, his lantern flashed on a form crouching in the snow. The baker looked down at his only son.

Lovel called his name and knelt and chafed the boy's hands. When he couldn't warm them, he began to weep. Suddenly Lovel's son raised his bloody head and extended his hand. "Look there, Father! That man on the river. It's not a man, its a wicked specter." He drew his hand across his brow to clear his sight of blood. "It seized me outside the store when I tried to speak with you and beat me 'til I fled. Beat me bloody."

Bending over the rock, the baker looked. There, under the dark sky, he saw a tall form muffled in a cloak, standing on a float of ice. The wind tossed back its cloak and threw off the beaver hat. Where the head should have been was a full Yule Moon. The wintry Hudson River took it out of sight momentarily. When the ice-pile reappeared, it was empty. "Father," gasped the boy tottering on his feet. "Give me the musket... help me up. Mother sent me to tell you to come home right away... one of the girls has... without your consent." And here he swooned, fell, and lay stiff and cold in the snow. On his lips hung the faintest of words. "Run away with a newcomer from England."

ONE

NOW COMES A GHOST STORY, the story of a boy who at the age of seven dreamed of looking at a grave.

It began this way: A little boy stood at a grave in the cemetery, the grave of his parent's. They were said to have taken their own lives. For this sin, he'd been told, the arms of his parents would grow out of the grave like monstrous plants that reached for the moon.

The boy waited by the grave, but nothing happened. He went home and begged his uncle to dig up the grave and find out where his parents were.

The uncle laughed. A door in the ground opened and he grabbed the boy and pulled him into the dark hole.

THERE WAS A CERTAIN CORNER AT SCHOOL that Christian Snow knew quite well, even better than the corridors and classrooms inside. He stood there a lot lately. Ever since the murders and the madness. No one else usually came in his corner. Some kids waited until the last second to get on their buses outside the main entrance, sitting on the benches or leaning on the concrete planters. Behind him were the school office windows, tinted so he couldn't see in.

Not long ago he walked home after school, and he was able to wander the streets of Windsor whenever he wanted to; now he couldn't even walk from the Middle School to the train shop by himself, and the train shop was in plain sight.

Christian's uncle picked him up exactly on time; it just felt like he was late. Randy said they needed gas and groceries. "Whatever," said Christian. He looked out his window as they drove past the train shop and over the Occanum Creek bridge. In 2006 the creek had risen and swept a house away; now the creek was reconstructed in an attempt to contain it.

Randy turned left on Chapel Street. To the right was the Bridge Street bridge where six years ago his parents were found dead on the bank of the Susquehanna River. He'd been seven-years-old. Nobody talked about it much, at least not to Christian. He figured they committed suicide and didn't ask. It was right then, as they made the right turn, that Christian realized Randy had been avoiding that bridge for the past six years. He looked at his uncle.

"What?" asked Randy.

"Nothing," he answered.

Gloria VanCoth was working the cash register in the Big M. She was a friend of his cousin Hilary, or second cousin, or whatever, and had been keeping tabs on him for his cousin's sake. Maybe it was because he was pretty much the only Snow left, besides his freaky cousin Arizona and his grandmother and great aunt, who he hadn't visited in six years. Christian knew that Hilary had been a two-year-old child when her mother died, so she barely got to know the Snow side of her family. Gloria smiled when she saw him.

"Christian, how was school? Don't look so gloomy. Hello, Randy."

"Hi, Gloria. How are you?" began Randy. He nodded toward Christian. "He's mad he can't walk home from school, but if my car was broke down then he'd be mad if he had to walk."

Christian flashed a glance at him, then he made a face. "I doubt that."

"We'll be back," Randy told Gloria, then headed toward the deli. "Don't go outside alone," said Christian as he followed, mocking his uncle's voice. "Watch out for strangers. Beware that turkey I shot for Thanksgiving."

Randy laughed, and said, "Very funny. Very creative." He pointed down the store aisle. "Now, why don't you go and create your menu for school lunch this week. Something besides Swedish Fish, okay?"

On the way home, Christian saw a man standing on a rock in Occanum Creek and it struck him as odd. The man stood at an off angle and his clothes didn't fit. "Look!" he said. Randy looked at him. "Nothing. Too late." Then, under his breath: "Beware of strangers."

At sometime before 5:00, Christian was sitting on the foot of his bed and looking out his bedroom window at nothing in particular, one arm on the sill, his chin resting on his fist. It was chilly here, he could feel a slice of early winter chill across his cheek and nose but it wasn't that bad. There was a trace of ice around the outer pane of glass and he could just see over its bottom edge. He had sat here for days after his parents died, barely seeing over the window sill then, just staring at the sky mostly. Once this spot at the window had been for mourning. But not now. Now it was just a familiar place.

It was almost dark. A car sped down Grove Street, its headlights sweeping over the house as if searching for prisoners. Shadows slipped across the yard like ghosts on skateboards. One in particular moved among the others. Whatever it was it moved quickly, low to the ground, like the rest of the shadows. Christian saw that it was a dog. It began to bark. Yellowish light glinted off—he couldn't tell—either teeth or saliva. Something else was in the yard; a man. He stood as still as a scarecrow.

Christian went out into the yard, figuring that a neighbor was trying to corral a loose dog. Something was retreating up the hill behind the house. The dog's fitful barking was moving farther off. In what was left of the daylight, Christian's breath looked like cigarette smoke. He heard movement behind him and he turned around.

The approaching figure stopped not much more than five paces away. Their breaths came by turns, rising in the cold air.

"Christian," a man's voice tried to say but the voice was hoarse. "Christian," it said again, plainer. "We have to talk, you and I."

Christian sniffed and said nothing.

"You're a sneaky kid, aren't you? I bet you're the one who's been looking in my windows at night. Did you get an eyeful?"

It was the guy next door, Arnold Dujanovich; Arnie, Randy called him. Christian was stunned.

"Someone," said Arnie, moving a step closer, "was following me. Was that someone you? If it was, I'll make sure you pay for your mischief!"

Christian shook his head before he suddenly flared into anger. "I don't know what you're talking about, you idiot."

Arnie Dujanovich began to back off. "Stay out of my yard!" he barked as he moved away.

"Hey, you're the one who's trespassing!" yelled Christian.

BODY AFTER BODY WAS FOUND in Windsor and Ouaquaga during the last days of November and the beginning of December. In a house on Main Street a woman's remains were discovered scattered across her kitchen floor. Apparently crazed by hunger, the woman's dog had eaten her face. Not far from her house was another in which a child was found strangled while innocently playing in a room. In a field along the river the body of Walter Connolly was discovered. The large logger, with a last, hopeless surge of strength, had tried to defend himself with his ax. Both the man's ax and arm were broken in two.

Only the truly brave or tragically foolish ventured outside alone. Police cars and police dogs were now a common sight. At the end of each day, Big M employees were escorted to their vehicles in the parking lot.

At 9:15 on December fourth Gloria VanCoth came home to a lit up house; she had turned on a half dozen lights before she left for work. Now she sat alone with Gary, spooked by every sound, inside the house and out. Besides locking the front door, she had blocked it from opening with a heavy living room chair.

The footsteps she thought she heard on the stairs couldn't be real. The dead were not walking in her house.

Gloria got up from the straight-backed chair, partially closed Gary's door behind her, and turned on another light. The stairs complained as she moved up them, just as they had a minute ago. On the top step she stared at a brown leaf that clung to the carpet. The door to the first bedroom was open, as Gloria looked inside her shadow stepped in to block the hall light.

A series of hollow raps alerted her to the second bedroom, her bedroom. This time her shadow didn't block the view, she watched in shock as a leathery-looking dead man struggled out from under her bed. Gloria blinked. There was nothing there, of course. Just her fear. It had forced her up the stairs and now it forced her back down.

In her well lit living room she stood helpless as her imagination ran wild. Gary's door was slowly opening. In the kitchen, two long-dead men wearing her husband's clothes were trying to move the heavy chair.

Gloria closed her eyes. She opened them and peeked in the coat closet, then stepped in to switch on the closet light. Her skin crawled before she felt the touch. Something wrapped around her neck, glided down her back.

Coats. They fell on top of her. Gloria stumbled to her knees and looked up.

There was no dead. The empty clothes hangers swung nervously, trying to tell her—that—something... *was*... there.

TWO

I T WAS SNOWING IN ALBANY. Hilary opened the door of her
father's bakery, the bell rang, and she stepped outside and
beheld a winter wonderland. The snowflakes falling on State
Street under the decorated streetlamps were tremendous, seeing
them Hilary though of parachutes, layers of them, floating in slow
motion. "More snow," she told herself. She grabbed her coat. She
began to shovel the storefront. Then, as she was shoveling, a
revelation fell on her like an avalanche.

It was here. At her father's bakery.

She didn't want to turn around, never wanted to. Whatever
haunted the Snow sisters was behind her as it always had been. Hilary
moved slowly, her head turning in a series of jerking degrees. She
caught a shapeless bulk with the edge of her vision.

Hilary faced the ghost who stood in her father's shop doorway.

She would try to explain it to Gloria, later, and would never find
the words. It was a half-ghost; the swirling snowflakes, they clung to
it, building onto it, completing it where it was lacking. A face stared
out from the whirling geometrics of the squall, the patterns too
complex. The face too terrible. Hilary screamed and ran out into the
four lanes of State Street.

BUT THERE WAS NO STREET.

She stood in a dark chamber, breathing rotten air. There was a wet movement. With the movement there was a voice.

Stop what you're doing, the voice echoed harshly. *Stop it right now.*

For a moment she was aware of only shock. Shock and darkness.

Don't you know you're killing her?

Recognition hurt her deeply; she realized this was real.

"Grandma!" she called.

AND THERE WAS NO ECHO.

Miserably, her voice was swallowed by the same stagnant clouds that supported a cradle moon. Her toes hung over the edge of a steep hill; the soft edge threatened to give out.

A hung moon spread light with implausible intensity on the village of Windsor below. An oily rain struck her coat, crawled in her scalp, dripped into her eyes. The cliff edge puddled and sank. Hilary tried to pull her feet free but the mud was too thick. That was when she noticed her shadow: It stood behind her, taller than Hilary, and bent. Looking down. Hilary saw the dark sphere of its head over her own.

Then the edge caved in and Hilary was pulled down, caught like a animal in the mud, down to the rocks and the village street. She closed her eyes. Nothing here could really hurt her. She would be all right, her shadow rode behind her and she clung to it as if it was her father.

(no)

No!

Nothing was real. The street—yes, she recognized it, it was Main Street in Windsor. But the cliff was not. The shadow... even the shadow was not.

The ghost was. That was hers.

THEN THERE WAS NO ILLUSION.

She was standing on the sidewalk in front of her father's bakery. Staring at the blood on her hands. It was her own blood, she found when she washed; her fingernails had cut half-moons in her palms. She set the store alarm, turned off the lights, locked the door and went home, wondering if she would see her father's shop again. It was the blood that finally forced her out of her house, which drove her back to Windsor. But the blood did not let her free. The stickiness became gelatinous between her fingers where it would not come off. She clutched the steering wheel harder.

"I'm coming," she whispered.

THREE

GLORIA WAS PUTTING AWAY SUPPER DISHES when she got a text from Hilary. She read the first part. Her face lit up. Hilary was packing her bags and coming back to Windsor. But Gloria read the second half and frowned, wondering what exactly was going on. WORRIED ABOUT THE SISTERS, read the text. The Snow sisters? Gloria glanced at the clock. It wasn't much past 8:00 and the chicken cacciatore on the countertop was still warm. Gloria thought for a minute, then threw on her coat, got her car keys and her oven mitts, and carried the Crock-Pot to the garage.

It was cold outside but not freezing, even though the evening news had said that snow was on the way. She was making a conscious effort not to think too much about the voluntary curfew as she put the Crock-Pot on the passenger seat and strapped the seat belt around it. After all, everyone was supposed to check in on their neighbors. Anyway, once she was in the car with the doors locked and the headlights on, she felt safe.

A minute later she was in the Snow driveway. Gloria left her lights on and got out of the car, walked quickly around it, then got the chicken cacciatore. On the way to the porch she glanced back at her car but was blinded by the headlights. Each porch step leaned at a different angle. Gloria tried to knock but she was holding the crock-

Pot. The thick oak door pushed open just from her effort. Gloria walked in.

There was a single lamp turned on in the front room. She smelled smoke, and heard fire crackle in the wood stove. She crossed the room and looked in the kitchen. It was a mess, pots and pans on the floor. Drawers hung open. Gloria quietly placed the Crock-Pot on the dirty stove. She wasn't sure why she was being quiet. Maybe she thought it might be better to surprise whoever else was in the house than get surprised.

Hands in her coat pockets, she walked upstairs and found the first room empty. The second door was shut. "Hello," she said softly. Then louder: "It's Gloria next door."

The door stuck, making an irritable splintering as it pushed in. When she picked up on the doorknob it swung smoother; she found the light switch. The first thing she saw was someone in bed.

"Hello? Are you awake?" Gloria moved closer to see who it was.

The thin, frail woman lying on her back with her arms above her head wasn't Edythe but she was horribly old looking. A thick bedspread covered her to her shoulders, exposing her neck and her face: her skin was a discolored mottle of gray and dark reddish-brown. "Amber? Amber Snow?" The old woman's mouth could have been any number of folds above the bony knob of her chin, her eyes were half-open, and looked sightless, like Gary's. It was Amber Snow and Gloria couldn't have been more surprised.

So she thought. Behind Amber Snow's head was a confusion of pillows. The old woman's arms were partially hidden in them, yet the rope that tied her hands to the bedposts was in plain sight. Gloria gasped and stepped back. Pure panic showed her details she had missed.

A small hatchet on the dresser; lengths of rope on the floor; two bare feet were sticking out from under the bed.

Without thinking, she stepped forward and pulled down the bedspread. Gloria blinked while her eyes focused on the bloody mess. Amber Snow's feet were gone.

"Jesus Christ!" screamed Gloria, and from somewhere deep in the house a baby began to cry.

Turn and run, she told herself. *Turn and run and get help.* But she couldn't leave the poor old woman tied as she was. Gloria turned and looked around.

There was the hatchet on the dresser. She picked it up…

The crying got closer.

… she picked it up, truly fascinated by the fact that before this moment she'd never held a hatchet in her hand. Untying knots was not something Gloria had a knack for, but chopping vegetables was, and a rope was no more than an overly fibrous carrot.

Ten chops each bedpost and it was done. Amber's arms never moved. Gloria stepped away from the bed; the crying now was very loud, it was right outside the room.

Gloria started toward the door and stifled a scream with the back of her hand. Arizona Snow was in the doorway. She was severely beautiful, dressed in a long loose black robe. In one arm she cradled a baby. It ceased crying as soon as it saw Gloria; it's wet eyes sparkled. The thing was milky-white, a soft, thick mass which clung to her arm. In her other hand, Arizona carried a long metal rod, pointed and barbed.

Gloria still held the hatchet.

"Arizona," she said in a rushed voice. "Your grandmother?"

Arizona stood deadly still. "You're trespassing," she said.

"But, what…"

Arizona's eyes became slits. She thrust the spear in Gloria's direction. Her nose puckered and she smiled. "What is it? It's a boy. He's the mound's child."

Gloria moved to the closet door where a broom leaned against the frame, knocking it over on the floor. The girl means to kill me, she thought.

What happened next took mere seconds: In a blur, Amber was out of the bed. With feet nothing more than flesh trailing stumps, she jerked forward with a cat's balance and hurled herself at Arizona.

Without hesitation Arizona stabbed her grandmother through the abdomen with the spear. Gloria was frozen to the spot.

When Arizona tried to pull the spear out of Amber's stomach it stuck. She tried again and this time she dropped the baby. The sound it made when it struck the floor was enough to break through Gloria's physical shock and she ran into the hall and down the stairs. A boy... a thing that sort of looked like a boy, dressed in clothes that didn't fit, as tall as a young teen, stood in the living room. "*Trespassing*," it hissed in a watery voice. It looked curiously at her as she opened the front door.

Gloria's car lights were on, the beams streaked with silver. It was just starting to snow. Because of the headlights, she didn't see the shadows moving in the driveway until it was too late.

"Is that you, Edythe?"

The night laughed in her face.

She glimpsed them, their faces whitely luminous on both sides of her car. They moved toward her. This time she screamed.

EDYTHE SNOW WAS BOUND TO THE TRUNK of the old pine behind the house, drifting in a place somewhere between consciousness and unconsciousness, when Gloria's scream woke her up. It took her a moment to remember what happened. During the birth of Arizona's fourth abomination, December's child, Arizona's first two droppings had tied her to the tree and left her to die. Where Amber's droppings had always wandered off to commit aimless acts of atrocities on the unsuspecting people of Windsor and Ouaquaga, these two remained nearby.

She had no feeling in her arms, but her feet worked. She was still standing up. And she was numb to the cold. She was thinking that she might have dreamed the scream when her night eyes spied someone running around the house who was not wearing her dead husband's clothes, who wore shoes on their feet. Edythe tried to call for help but wasn't sure what came out. The figure came toward her.

It was Gloria VanCoth, her eyes wide with confusion and fear. Edythe's neighbor was holding a hatchet like it was a soup ladle.

"Oh my god, how long have you been here?" whispered Gloria, looking behind her at the dark and the snow. Edythe shook her head.

Gloria paused, but only briefly. Then she moved behind the pine. Ten chops and the rope fell from the tree.

"Take my arm."

"Thank you, Gloria."

"We'll go to my house. I left my phone there. We can call for help."

"I'm so sorry. There's nothing that you can do."

They made it through the tree line to the depression in the ground that was the spot of the original Snow house. Gloria's yard started on the other side of it. At the bottom Edythe stopped and let go of Gloria.

"This is far enough. *They* won't let us go any further."

Gloria turned. She saw three figures at the edge of the depression.

"They have us trapped," said Edythe, her teeth chattering.

"Who? What are they?"

"They're Arizona's droppings, Arizona and the mound."

Gloria shook her head and looked at Edythe like she wasn't making any sense. She asked, "Arizona and what?"

"The ghost in the mound."

FOUR

AFTER A LONG DAY HELPING HIS UNCLE install a new metal roof on a garage, Christian went to bed early, worn out, and fell at once into a deep sleep. Almost immediately, he was awakened and attempted to sit up, but could not, and was startled to see his mother standing close by. As he tried to speak she smiled at him, spoke his name, then, leaning down, seemed to kiss him; then drew away a little and said: "You're being watched."

The furnace kicked on. Christian sat up in bed and hugged his knees. He couldn't remember the dream he'd just had, but it left him with the feeling of being watched. Except for the furnace, the house was quiet. He moved to his familiar spot on the foot of his bed and sat there. Tomorrow was Sunday, and the six year anniversary of his parent's deaths; perhaps *they* had been watched, there under the bridge. Christian yawned, reached up, and pulled aside the curtain to look outside. A face, colorless and swollen, peered in at him.

Christian cried out loud and leapt back, falling off the bed. He heard a crash in the house.

His uncle came through his bedroom door and rushed into the room. Christian didn't even notice that Randy was naked.

"What's wrong?" he said sleepily, anxiously.

Christian pointed to the window.

"Outside! Someone's right outside!"

78

They both looked out. It had begun to snow. The first accumulation, according to the news. There seemed to be nobody outside.

"Go back to bed," his uncle told him. "We'll check things out in the morning."

HILARY PULLED INTO GLORIA'S DRIVEWAY at 12:22 Sunday morning. She hadn't heard from her friend since their original texting, but a few house lights were on. Gloria's car wasn't parked outside, but it was snowing. She assumed it was in the garage.

Hilary knocked and tried the handle; the door was unlocked. It was unnerving, walking alone through someone else's house after midnight. These late night shadows were the secretive kind and they laid low on Gloria's carpet in private clusters. The shadows, if she let her imagination get the best of her, seemed to scheme with one another as she cautiously moved past; they slid behind the partially closed coat closet door, they merged under the table when she looked in the kitchen.

The shadows jumped when she called Gloria's name. Hilary took a deep breath and called again. With a nervous dread she looked in Gloria's husband's room.

Gary was sitting bolt upright in his chair.

"It's just me," said Hilary in a half-whisper. "Hilary. I know it's late but Gloria's expecting me."

The shadows conspired here, too. They gave Gary's bandaged face an emotion which he couldn't have had: a menacing glee. Hilary felt a chill run up her back and she shuddered.

She went upstairs, called Gloria's name again, then looked in every room. She went back downstairs.

Gary was not in his chair.

Hilary backed into the living room, tripping over her own feet. "Gloria!" she nearly screamed and heard the fear in her voice.

She heard a noise behind her; shifting weight on old floorboards. She knew it was Gary. Hilary was too afraid to turn around.

GLORIA SAT AT THE SNOW KITCHEN TABLE shivering uncontrollably despite the fact that it was warm in the house and feeling had returned to her fingers. Arizona Snow was there, pacing the kitchen and glancing at Gloria with a rabid annoyance. The things that weren't men but were in the shapes of men stood silently behind her.

Gloria closed her eyes and tried to picture in her mind the self-defense class she had taken years ago in Klump Park. She couldn't. When the things that Edythe called Arizona's droppings had begun to move down into the depression, Edythe and Gloria ran in different directions. They caught Gloria as she was climbing out, and she had tried to fight, but uselessly. Gloria thought that Edythe might have somehow gotten away.

Gloria opened her eyes. Arizona was walking to the front room, to the picture window alcove, heavily curtained against the cold winter nights. There was an old baby cradle in the alcove, sitting directly in Gloria's view from the kitchen table. She watched as Arizona bent down and picked up the baby. Then Arizona carried the child into the kitchen.

Gloria was concentrating hard on not looking at the baby in her arms. She kept her gaze on the alcove and at first the movement there seemed disconnected to what was going on around her; then Gloria slowly realized that she was the only one who noticed that someone hid behind the curtains. The curtains parted, just slightly. It was Edythe. The old woman had not gotten away. She had snuck back into the house. Arizona, pacing again, mistook the look on Gloria's face.

"I never wanted this life, you know," she said to Gloria. Her eyes smoldered with indignation. "I never asked to be a Snow. I never asked to live in these godforsaken hills in this godforsaken town."

Gloria was surprised to hear her own voice.

"You *killed* your grandmother. You killed her right in front of me."

Arizona nodded. "She would have killed me. It had to be, just like Edythe will have to be. My grandmother told me the carvings would take the mark off my skin. She lied. Did those two old women think the ghost in the mound would keep them alive forever? Then they were mistaken."

Gloria stared at her. "I don't understand," she whispered.

"Of course you don't, you're not a Snow woman." Arizona set the child on the floor. "He's learning to walk."

The swollen toddler walked with short, unsteady steps across the kitchen and front room to its cradle, where it dropped to the floor with a wet sound. The little cradle rocked as it climbed in.

"Let me go," pleaded Gloria. "Let me go home and... we'll never speak about this again. I promise."

Arizona sneered. "No." She turned and opened the refrigerator. She looked in. "I just want a little quiet time before... well, just before. I'm afraid that I'm going to have to," she smiled, "evict you."

Gloria started to stand up. The thing behind her clamped a hand around the back of her neck and squeezed. Gloria sat back in the chair. Movement none of the others could see caught her attention. Edythe came out from behind the curtains with a pair of shears in her hand. She bent over the cradle and began to slash and slice with the open shears without making a sound.

HILARY WALKED OUT OF GLORIA'S HOUSE through the front door, not daring to turn around. She heard only her own footsteps on the porch, down the steps.

Her Jeep was gone.

She allowed herself to glance once behind her, seeing a dark and empty yard, and took a deep breath. Then Hilary followed the car tracks in the freshly-fallen snow. She found it, just off the other side of the road in the treeline.

"Damn it," breathed Hilary. She had to step through a stand of white trees to reach her door. When she pulled it open the interior light came on. Gary was sitting in the driver's seat.

GLORIA FROZE when Arizona suddenly rushed toward the cradle. Perhaps it was the dripping from underneath that gave it away. She lifted the child in pieces and stepped away.

"*Where are you, old woman!*" exploded Arizona. The man-thing behind Gloria rushed forward, ripping the curtains apart one by one until Edythe was revealed, still holding the glistening shears. The large man-thing locked his arm around Edythe's thin neck and lifted her off the floor.

Gloria stood and took a step. But not in time.

The other man-thing hit Gloria hard with the back of his hand. It was almost a casual gesture, but the force of the big man's hand knocked her backwards, and she fell over the chair. Her head struck the kitchen table; she almost lost consciousness. She tasted blood in her mouth.

The thing that had Edythe snapped her neck like it was a twig. She dropped the shears. Her head lolled back. She looked at Gloria, a final tear rolled down her wrinkled forehead, and her eyes went dead.

Then, mercifully, consciousness finally fled, and Gloria's world went dark.

HILARY WAS RUNNING UP THE SNOW COVERED ROAD, running away from the terrifying sight of Gary, running away from her Jeep. She realized her bag was in her car, along with her phone, but she didn't stop. Four minutes later, she was climbing the Snow sister's sagging front porch. She knocked on the door and, when no one answered, let herself in.

She saw her grandmother lying motionless in the front room and rushed to her, bending over her to see if she was breathing. Edythe was obviously dead. Then, lifting her eyes, she stared into the kitchen and saw Gloria. She, too, was lying on the floor, but a groaning sound was coming from her lips.

At that very moment Gary, dressed in wet, partially frozen sweatpants and sweatshirt, appeared in the front doorway. His bandages were hanging from his face. His blind eyes were now cold and dark and hard. Hilary had time to take two steps backward before he charged toward her, reaching for her, grabbing her with a strong grip and pulling her forward. His other hand, knotted into a fist, hit her between the eyes, knocking her to the floor. She struggled to get up. Another punch to the side of her head left her in a motionless stupor.

With an uncanny strength, he hoisted Hilary to his shoulder and carried her out the open door, around the Snow house, and into the dark trees. Snowflakes fell on Hilary's face and melted. Gary stumbled through the woods. He climbed the miniature hill, pulled up the sod, and dumped a semiconscious Hilary into the mound.

FIVE

CHRISTIAN WAS UP BEFORE THE SUNRISE at 7:15. Two inches of snow had blanketed the Susquehanna valley overnight. When dawn came, the snow lay white and smooth, marked only by small animal and bird tracks. Randy stood next to Christian outside, under Christian's bedroom window, and both looked down at the footprints in the snow. They were 6 inches long, 2 3/4 inches wide, and 12 inches apart, and appeared to have been made by a creature walking upright on two legs. The prints began under Christian's window, zigzagged through the back yard and then followed the old tractor trail up the steep hill.

"What are they?" asked Christian.

"I don't know."

"Are they human?"

Randy shrugged. "I don't know," he said and paused. "There's no tracks leading up to your window, there's only tracks leading away."

"What does that mean?"

"That whatever made these tracks was standing here while it snowed."

Christian was silent, not knowing what to say.

Randy turned to him. "Chris, go in the house, dress warm, and get your rifle."

"What are we going to do?"

"We're going to arm ourselves and follow these tracks."

The trail of mysterious footprints led Randy and Christian up the hill and into dense woods, across a small white field, over rock walls, and in and out of thickets. Eventually, they led to the power lines, and turned north on the snow covered dirt maintenance road.

"Is there a reason we're not stepping on the tracks?" asked Christian, readjusting his gun strap and jumping to the other side of the footprints in the snow.

"Not really." Randy glanced behind him. "Step on them if you want to."

"No thanks."

The tracks turned east and zigzagged again, sometimes following forgotten tractor trails, sometimes through shallow ravines and snow covered undergrowth. Near a farm the footprints led into an old shed with a dilapidated roof and out the other side. Whatever made them had gone through a six-inch-diameter hole.

"What the hell?" said Randy. He walked back around the shed, stared at the hole in the wall, then retraced his steps outside. "You see this? *This* is why we're not stepping on the tracks."

Christian hesitated when his uncle began to push forward into the thick trees. "Do you want to turn around and go back home?" Randy asked softly. "I know that today is the... well, I know what today is."

"It's not like these footprints are going to lead us under the bridge, Randy," said Christian harshly. "We're walking in the opposite direction."

"That's not what I meant, Chris."

"No. We're going to follow the tracks. So, let's get going."

The sun was shinning but it was thirty degrees and there was an added chill under the trees. Twenty minutes after they'd left the shed, the woods lightened and they stepped out of the trees and into a farmer's field that stretched as far as they could see to the north and south. Route 79 and the river snaked through the valley far below, pristine in the newly fallen snow. The footprints were not as deep in the open field where the snow was partly hard-frozen. In some places deer tracks crisscrossed them.

They could see a large barn a hundred yards down the hill. The footprints headed straight for it. Christian moved his rifle back to the other shoulder and started to walk a little faster. Randy grabbed his arm.

"Remember, Chris, being on somebody's land, especially carrying guns, is not cool."

"Hey! Hey you two!"

They turned. The farmer was an impressive bulk of a man, dressed in heavy boots, vest, suspenders, and a wide-brimmed hat. His white beard was frosted from his breath.

"Oh, great," whispered Randy. "Let me do the talking."

"Are you two following the tracks?" the farmer hollered.

Randy jogged up to him while Christian lagged behind. "Yeah. They start at our house," explained Randy, gesturing southward with his hand.

The farmer shook his bearded head. "No shit," he said. "Well, come take a look at this."

They walked across the expanse of snow toward the farmhouse. The footprints went in and out of the barn, through an enclosed garden, on the doorstep, and then the farmer pointed upward. The tracks went over the house's rooftop.

On the other side of the house the tracks continued without displacing the snow, moving on as if the house had not been any kind of impediment. The farmer pointed toward the back of the house. "They go through those apple trees," he said, "and then back up the hill, it looks like. By the way, my name's Chester. Last name Vail."

Randy extended his hand. "I'm Randy Devon. And this is my nephew, Christian Snow."

The big farmer raised an eyebrow.

"Do you mind if we continue walking on your land?" asked Randy.

"Mind if I tag along?" asked Vail. He patted his girth and grinned. "I don't eat much."

86

"Not at all," said Randy. "The more, the merrier."

Christian rolled his eyes.

"THE DEVIL HAS WALKED IN WINDSOR."

Chester Vail said the words with wide eyes.

The creature, or whatever it was that had made the tracks, appeared to have crawled through a drainpipe, leaving tracks at both ends. "Believe me now?" asked Randy. He had told Vail about the hole in the abandoned shed.

"I wouldn't have," said the farmer. "Not if I hadn't seen it with my own eyes."

Eventually, they were led into the woods again and back to the power lines. A fox followed them for a time. The mention of the devil caused Christian to see things; black tree trunks, half-hidden by the snow, looked like petrified men.

Vail lit a pipe. He turned to Christian. "You know where this power line corridor goes, don't you, young man?"

"Somewhere north. Ouaquaga, I suppose."

Vail blew a long cloud of smoke. "You're a Snow, aren't you? It's a direct line, straight as an arrow, from town to Snow land."

"I suppose so."

After what seemed a long time to Christian, the tracks left the maintenance road and headed into deep woods. It was hard going for all three of them, but Vail had it the hardest. The big man began breathing hard. Finally he stopped and leaned against a logged tree. The footprints they were following continued down a path through snow-covered ferns. In front of him was a monstrous dead pine.

"This," he said, "is where we cross into Snow land."

Randy stepped under the branches of the ancient tree. He looked up and asked, "Does any one else smell smoke?"

AFTER PONDERING THE BODIES ON THE FLOOR—her shredded newborn, a broken Edythe Snow, Gloria from next door, and, of course, her dead grandmother upstairs—Arizona realized that she needed a drink. Gloria's car was parked in the driveway still running, so she took it, leaving her Pontiac in the garage. The liquor store had closed hours ago. Arizona broke open the back door. She knew she had forty-five seconds before the alarm. The hot cinnamon whiskey she liked was on a lower shelf in the back of the store; she took two and was back in Gloria's car when the alarm went off. Not a soul was around.

She drove in circles for four hours, drinking, laughing. On a back road, she pulled to the side just before daybreak. When she woke up it was approaching noon. Arizona opened the car door and threw up, then she buckled her seat belt and drove back to the Snow house.

Everything was as Arizona had left it.

She stepped over Edythe's body on her way to the wood stove. While November's child stood next to her watching, Arizona collected kindling and stacked it teepee-like over wadded newspaper. She started a fire, but not in the stove.

Arizona started a fire in the middle of the front room floor, and then quickly retrieved the metal box filled with money she knew was hidden in Edythe's room, threw her clothes in her suitcase, collected last month's child, and left the house to burn.

HEMMED IN BY A GROUP OF TREES whose limbs were disfigured by ugly cankers, Chester Vail reached into his vest pocket and pulled out a small bottle of ginger flavored brandy. He held it up in front of him. "Care for a swig or two?" he asked Randy. "It's medicinal, you know, against the cold."

Randy shook his head. "I'm not really a brandy drinker," he said, stepping carefully to the other side of the mysterious tracks. "And I usually don't drink this early in the day."

Vail shrugged. "One swallow doesn't make a summer."

"I'm not sure I'm following you."

"A swallow is a bird," Christian slowly explained. "He's saying that one drink doesn't make you an alcoholic."

"Okay, you're right," said Randy, smiling. He took the bottle. As he took a drink Vail turned to Christian who was busy kicking a tree to get the snow off his boots.

"How about you, young man? Care for a swig?"

Randy handed Vail the ginger brandy. "*He* definitely doesn't drink."

"One swallow doesn't make a summer," said Christian. He pulled out a bag from his coat pocket, opened it, and tossed a handful of red Swedish Fish in his mouth. He held out the bag to Randy. "Want some?"

"Sure," said Randy.

"Good. Then you can hold the bag."

Suddenly they were out of the thick trees and Vail pointed at the ground on their left. "Someone else has been walking in these woods," he said. Soon the other set of human tracks intersected the ones they were following. When they rounded the side of the hill they were confronted with a further complication: more footprints, many of them. And that wasn't all; the smell of smoke was becoming more powerful.

"Something's burning," said Christian. He looked up at the treetops. "Something close."

Vail stuffed the brandy back in his vest pocket. "Looks like a clearing up ahead."

There was someone in the clearing. A girl with disheveled hair stood by herself, staring at a miniature hill in the center of the clearing. "I know who that is," whispered Randy and she turned and looked at them. Randy looked at her legs.

"Oh shit," he said.

ONE SWALLOW DIDN'T MAKE A SUMMER, but a single moment could last a young man's lifetime. Seconds ticked by in a series of snapshots: It was Christian's cousin, Arizona Snow, who stood in the clearing. Christian recognized confusion on her face, and he understood that she had just stepped into the clearing herself. Then he saw that she was standing in a campfire. Two men—or whatever they were—swayed like trees in the wind. Christian could not take his eyes off them. They were deathly pale, and bloated. Their eyes too large, too wet. Their clothes didn't fit them.

There were others in the snow covered clearing. Indian ghosts, half seen against the bright white. They were wearing deer hides; some men had shaved heads, and stretched ears decorated with silver. A woman on the miniature hill was wrapped in a blanket and held a wooden carving and a knife. They were all in disagreement. An Indian in a tall gray hat gestured toward the black smoke billowing above the trees, darkening the sky next to the noon sun.

One of the bloated men separated from the trees and seized Vail by the arm, bending the big farmer backwards. Vail's arm was forced out of its socket and he screamed in pain. Then the thing wrapped its hands around Vail's neck and squeezed and twisted. The Indians moved past Arizona, through her in fact, and up onto the mound; when this caused Arizona to cry out in terror, the bloated thing hesitated.

Randy's gun fired. The blast of the gun echoed over the hill. It took four more shots to take the thing down, but it was too late. Vail dropped to the ground, his tongue strangled out and lying on his chin. One of his eyes hung on his cheek.

The other bloated man attacked Randy, yanking the rifle from his hands, violently flinging him to the ground.

Christian emptied his pump-action rifle into its chest.

It fell, yet like the other, it wasn't dead. On their knees in the snow, they began to slowly crawl toward him.

LIGHT PENETRATED HER EYELIDS, waking her slowly. Her body ached, and a trail of dry blood ran from the corner of her mouth to the kitchen floor.

Where am I? thought Gloria. *Why am I on the floor?* Her eyes focused on the light. She realized she was watching Arizona light a fire. Gloria lay motionless as smoke began to fill the front room. She waited while Arizona went upstairs, came back down with a suitcase in her hand, and called her creature to her. As soon as Arizona was out the door, Gloria began to cough. She stood up too quickly, falling back to one knee.

She slowly stood and walked through the front room holding her breath. Hand clamped over her nose and mouth, she peeked out the front door. There was no one in sight. Her car was gone. She stumbled to the corner of the garage, scanning the trees behind the house, and saw Arizona moving up the hill into the woods. Gloria turned and ran down the driveway, stopping when she saw Hilary's Jeep in the ditch on the other side of the road. It was empty. Leaning against the open driver's seat door was the spear that Arizona had used to kill Amber Snow.

ARIZONA FELT TWO THINGS when the phantom Indians moved through her and then climbed the mound: fear and fury. She literally felt the betrayal crawling across her skin. Her two adult offspring had fallen to their hands and knees and were now writhing on the ground, oozing watery blood in the snow. Her cousin Christian and his uncle were backing away from them, trying to reload their guns. Gloria watched them climb the mound, following the phantoms.

"Stand up and kill them!" she shrieked at her children.

And then Arizona heard a woman's scream coming from the mound.

WHY RANDY WAS FOLLOWING THE INDIANS to the top of the miniature hill while reloading his rifle, Christian didn't know; maybe it was to give them an advantage over the bloated men, or whatever they were, that were crawling toward them in the snow. But the bloated men stopped. Christian watched the phantom Indians, no more than projections in the daylight, climb down into a dark hole in the snowy moundtop. Christian glanced at his cousin. Arizona was running around the clearing in a fit of rage.

And then the scream. It momentarily rooted Christian's legs to the spot. A woman was fighting her way up out of the hole as the Indians were trying to enter it. It was Hilary. Christian tried to step forward to help her, but his legs wouldn't let him.

Randy's legs worked, though. The last Indian had vanished into the mound, dragging the screaming Hilary with him, and Randy, tossing his rifle at Christian's feet, ran to the center of the mound and half jumped, half slid into the hole.

GLORIA WATCHED FROM THE EDGE OF THE CLEARING, too terrified to step out from the trees. The things that resembled men but weren't, were not getting up from the ground, even after Arizona's raging insistence. When Gloria heard the words *Kill them*, she dared a few steps into the clearing. Then she heard a scream that she knew was Hilary's, a scream of pure terror. When it finally stopped, she ran toward the miniature hill, ran toward Arizona, ran toward the things on the ground. She held the spear in front of her, gripping it tightly in her white-knuckled hands. She slipped in the snow, regained her footing, and stopped when Arizona turned around.

There was something different about Arizona's face. She looked shell shocked instead of hostile—panic, laced with rage, which were causing tremors throughout her entire body.

"How dare you, you *bitch*!" she spat at Gloria, not four feet from the bloody point of the spear. "How dare you come here! You are *not family*!"

"Don't come any closer," Gloria told her in a hoarse voice. "Where is Hilary?"

"*You are not a Snow!*" Arizona screamed. She raised her arms as if intending to break Gloria's neck. She wasn't wearing a coat and her attention suddenly turned to her exposed arms. They were turning color.

It moved across her skin like a finger painting in progress, a finger painting of livid bruises, a purple so deep it surely stained her bones. Arizona's hands and arms were covered in an instant, it lept from under her blouse collar and up her neck the next. On her face, it swirled like deep red blood in a drain, even coloring her eyes, until only her bared teeth remained white.

And Arizona saw it all, she saw it in the shock on Gloria's face, and reflected in her wide eyes.

"It brought you here, you know," Arizona said, slowly. "It brought you *all* here." Arizona's quacking stopped. Her fear was subsiding. Her full rage was coming back. "And it can have you."

Gloria shook her head. Her mouth silently opened and closed. Then she pleaded: "What have you done to Hilary?"

"But it can't have me," said Arizona, ignoring her. "Not any more."

She took a quick step forward. Gloria tightened her grip on the spear and braced herself, then Arizona rushed toward her, thrusting herself onto the barbed spear point, and impaled herself below the collar bone. Forced backwards, Gloria fell, the blunt end of the spear breaking her ribs.

CHRISTIAN STARED INTO THE HOLE AND SAW PURE DARKNESS.

"Randy?" he called, his voice shaky. He tried again. "Randy! Hilary, are you in there?"

No answer. Above him, the blue sky had turned gray, and the sun went out as if blocked by a giant standing over him.

"Randy, answer me!"

Christian gave himself no time to think. He sat down in the snow, placed his feet in the hole, and lowered himself into the darkness.

SIX

GLORIA TIED TO SIT UP AND SCREAMED IN PAIN, so she lay where she was in the snow, only able to turn her head. A motionless Arizona lay next to her. She wasn't sure how long she laid there, the sun had disappeared behind thick clouds or smoke. When she finally felt frozen through, she tried again, this time rolling on her stomach and slowly getting on her knees. She thought she would pass out. It hurt to breath. Gloria forced herself to her feet and waited for the pain to subside. It didn't.

During that time, the very ground below her moaned, and a dark hole had opened up at the edge of the field. She barely acknowledged it as real. It took her nearly twenty minutes just to get up the mound. On the top she collapsed to her hands and knees. She rested, then crawled, following the footprints in the snow to the center of the mound.

SHE KNELT AT THE HOLE FOR A LONG TIME; gazing into it took away her pain. The longer she looked, the deeper she seemed to see. A face appeared in the hole. The face was the color of dirt and mud. The eyes were black until the daylight hit them. Then they turned dusty blue. The thing clawed its way upward. Gloria could hear its breath, a sharp, hissing sound that rose and swelled. The features of this being were frozen in a wide-eyed, openmouthed grimace as if screaming in pain. Gloria squeezed her eyes shut; to look on it was instant death. The creature began to call her name; it reached for her.

GLORIA RECOGNIZED THAT VOICE. Her eyes flashed open. She reached her arms down into the hole as far as they would go. And pulled up Hilary, so covered by mud and dirt that it clothed her naked body. Randy came next, nearly unrecognizable. His boots were gone, replaced by blood mixed with mud. A minute later Christian Snow pushed himself out of the hole. Like the others, his eyes were wild, and he was covered with the dirt from the mound.

EARLY SPRING 2024

NOW COMES A GHOST STORY, the life of a miserable young man who at the age of thirteen was drawn to a little hole in the ground, and who never really knew what drew him there. Christian told the story just once, on his twenty-first birthday. It was a week and a half after Hurricane Michael doused the East Coast. And even before Michael, it had been a wet summer in much of the Northeast. The Susquehanna and its tributaries were raging out of control after the remnants of the tropical storm dumped heavy rain on the already soggy village of Windsor.

The end began this way: Gloria turned off East Windsor Road, drove down the steep incline, and across the unplanted corn field toward Christian's cottage to implore him to get out, to beg if she had to. The lowest section of the road was flooded; she drove her boyfriend's Ford truck slowly through the water. At the deepest point the water came over the hood.

The cottage was right on the river bank. Gloria parked the truck, got out, and watched the swollen Susquehanna flow by. The swirling brown water was still rising. It took Christian several minutes to answer the door, though she could plainly hear him inside. When he finally opened the door Gloria smelled alcohol.

She smiled, "Happy birthday, Chris," she said. He let her inside. "How is Randy?"

"He had another stroke. He doesn't know who I am any more."

"I'm so sorry."

"I can't believe you drove down here," he said dryly. "Let me pour you a drink."

"No, I can't. I'm driving Pete's truck."

Christian staggered. "One swallow doesn't make a summer."

Gloria laughed. "What?"

"Nothing. Hey, it's my twenty-first, have a drink with me."

"One drink," she said. She eyed his glass. "What are you drinking?"

"Whiskey." He took her coat and Gloria sat down on the couch.

"That's why your eyes look a little glassy," she observed. "Is that why you're not answering your phone?"

He grinned. "Sort of," he told her. "And I'm not leaving. That's why you're really here."

"*And* it's your birthday."

Christian put ice in a glass and added apple flavored whiskey and soda. More whiskey than soda. He handed her the glass.

Gloria could hear the swollen river outside. Branches were snapping, trees were falling; she took a drink and it was good.

"But Christian, you have to leave. Just until the water goes down."

He shook his head. "I want to tell you."

Gloria hesitated. "Tell me what?"

"I'll tell you the truth." Christian downed his drink. He started to make another. "I want to tell you what I saw in the mound. I want to tell you what happened to Gary."

Gloria stirred uneasily on the couch. "I told you before. He's gone, and I don't think I want to know any more than that."

"But I want to tell you."

If Gloria had attempted to stand up, she wouldn't have been able to, her legs had gone numb. She took a long drink.

He began with the things he and Randy had shot to death eight years ago behind Edythe Snow's house. Arizona's droppings, Gloria had called them. There had been another one in the clearing that day, a smaller one; it had gotten away.

Gloria stared at him. "And Amber's before Arizona," she said.

"Yes, Amber's droppings, too. They still wander the hills of Windsor." Christian started to pace the room. "It felt like shooting a person. It wasn't a man, but it felt like I was shooting a man. And I was okay with it."

Gloria looked away at the coffee table. On it was an assortment of candles and flashlights. She remembered that the power was out. The sun would be going down soon.

"And when I lowered myself into that hole, I was okay with that. I really didn't believe I would be coming back."

She looked up. "Coming back?"

"From the mound. It was like... there's a throat in the mound and it swallowed us."

HE TOLD HER THAT HE PANICKED when he began to slip. He tried to hold on to something but it was so narrow he couldn't move his arms. Then the light was gone. Dirt was in his eyes and in his mouth. He was trapped in a dark hole, forever. Slipping downwards. Swallowed by Windsor, swallowed by a pulsing layer of earth that needed his sacrificial blood.

As he slipped further, the throat widened as if to accommodate him and he was able to move his arms. He felt stone in the throat. Around him were rings of stone laid flat, and he stopped himself from sliding on them. He clung there in the total darkness. After a while he may have forgot why he was there; he was unable to tell if his eyes were open or closed, he slipped and for a moment he thought he was falling upward. His wrist slammed against rock. He held on. He remembered his uncle. They were in the ground together.

What seemed to be the bottom of the shaft was not far below. Creeping on hands and knees at first, and then proceeding upright, Christian moved forward with nothing but blind desperation. He had a terrifying feeling that something was following him, about to reach for him; he took one step, then another. He *did not* stop or turn around. His fear stood tall behind him.

One more step—and nothing happened. Two more—and the sheer concentration of walking in the dark nearly caused him to loose his balance. His mind pulsed a steady signal, a signal to run, but the impulse was frozen in the chill of his spine.

Christian stumbled a final step, kicking into what sounded like a large tin can. He held his breath, thinking that it was strange how under the ground the darkness moved like wind. The dark played a delusion, not in front of but behind his eyes. A face, leering and nefarious. Below a large white forehead were eyes big as hen's eggs; pupils like black points; deformed ears, bent away from the skull. The face of Arizona's dropping.

"I shot you," whispered Christian. The mirage vanished yet the darkness was alive. It was getting ready to pounce. The darkness whispered back with a voice like a winter's wind.

Like a cold breath.

Trembling.

Darkness.

And an echo. Or the sound of two heartbeats.

Allowing curiosity to steal a little of the fear, Christian got down on his knees and felt the darkness at his feet. It was not a tin can.

He could not have been any more stunned if he had found his own carcass dead and stiff on the hard, cold floor. The lantern felt unbroken beneath his crazed, inquiring fingers. It felt like a kerosene lantern, and though it seemed too light, it ignited a dubious ray of hope in his heart.

No, it wasn't going to work; he knew that, with every fiber of his disbelieving existence, he knew it wouldn't work. No luck in the world—

It's a present, Chris. It's an early birthday present.

It was in the shape of a kerosene lantern, but it wasn't. It was battery powered. He felt the button on the lantern's side and pushed it.

The lantern that was not going to work worked. Christian thought it was the brightest lantern he had ever seen in his life. He found himself in a small subterranean room that was not much more than six feet high at its highest point, a room that was partially natural, partially man-made. Stretched out full-length on the stone floor was a skeleton with a old wooden carving that had rolled out of bony hands still seeking, it seemed, to clutch it fast. One skeleton after another came into his light, and Christian looked into their faces, eaten away by time, but still recognizable as such, the eye sockets empty, noses gone, mouths twisted into terrible smirks. Flesh still clung to some of the bones. Many wore silver jewelry and shell beads; and many had rotted away almost completely, crumbling to dust. Scattered among them were animal shaped carvings, some looked old, yet some looked new.

There was one part of the chamber that would not be illuminated. Christian cautiously moved forward a few steps, crushing a desiccated skull beneath his foot—and saw what looked like a passageway. He set the lantern down in the low opening and tried to peer into the darkness.

"Randy!" he shouted. His echo, it sounded captured, entombed. "Are you in there?"

He waited while the echo subsided, watching as the dust from the crushed skull, tiny bright specks in the halogen light, drifted in and out of the passageway's opening. For a moment he questioned his own sanity, then he remembered hearing that some caves actually breathed.

The shout finally died in the far distance in a faint echo that resembled a ripple of mocking laughter. Christian listened for an answer. He could feel the inhale and exhale against his face. It tousled his hair. Beyond any doubt, the cave was breathing.

Trying to control his fear, Christian began moving stiffly down the tunnel. After several minutes he had to stoop; the passage steepened to a forty-five degree angle. A little later and he had to go on hands and knees. His progress was slow. Then, at last, Christian found himself at the other end of the tunnel and he stood up, holding the lantern out in front of him. He was looking at a vast cavern, the roof so high as to be invisible, and the walls soaring up into darkness. The floor slopped upward to the left side. On his right it slopped down to a ten foot round pit filled with what looked like water. He could see an irregular shape near it.

"Randy?"

The echo was frightful.

Your mother's here, said a cold touch to his cheek. He turned and saw her. Then she was gone, though gradually, like a flower wilting and dropping from the stem. Someone tapped his shoulder. He turned, expecting to see his father. He saw Randy instead, thirty feet away, behind a pillar amid a jumble of fallen rocks. Christian hurried toward his uncle, calling his name, when a horrible sound began in the remote distance, a ghostly roar that drew rapidly near with louder and louder throbs of sound. Christian didn't know whether it was an echo of a noise or the noise itself.

Randy remained motionless, his face expressionless, his eyes unblinking. Christian could not get him to let go off the rock pillar. "Randy, for Christ's sake, let go."

Christian set the lantern down, but trying to pry Randy's fingers free was useless. And the pillar was loose, some of the fallen rocks moved under his feet.

"Randy god damn it, help me!"

Something was wrong. It was his words. Their echo.

It did not die down.

Christian picked up the lantern and looked up, searching, but couldn't see passed his cocoon of light.

He held the lantern higher. The gray floor slopped down to the pit. Still holding the light above his head, he turned to Randy. Stepped closer to him.

"I don't know what's happening," he whispered and felt the caves breath blow in his hair.

I don't know what's happening.

I don't know what's happening.

The lantern was ungently knocked from his hand.

I don't know—what's happening.

Christian was lifted into the air. Hands he couldn't see carried him to the black pit and dropped him in.

HE LAY THERE, IN THE SLIMY POOL, distantly aware of nearby light though not interested in where it came from. Swallowing a mouthful, he gagged and tried to push himself up and out of it. His hand was caught in algae or seaweed or something. He opened his eyes, distantly aware of his two friends—one on each side of him: the light and his shadow. The lantern light reached toward him, including him in its dazzling orb; his shadow stretched away, moving when he did, resting when he rested.

A mummified figure sat in front of him, not the whole body but the upper part of it, its calcified arms stretched out, its head bowed. Billions of waterdrops carrying limestone sediment had, over the countless ages, formed a drapery of glittering stone, an imperishable hood over its hidden skull. The lower part of the body had rotted and jellied together into a formless, liquid-like mass that filled the bow shaped pit in the cavern floor.

With eyes as glazed as his thoughts he looked down at his hand, lifting it from the dark slime. Blondish weeds, soft as moss, were entwined in his fingers. He pulled, and a head bobbed up out of the thick water. A head that spoke with the voice of a thousand dribbling water drops. Even through the fog in his head he recognized it.

Hilary's head.

It was Hilary's head.

HILARY COUGHED UP a great deal of black muddy slime. It ran for a long time out of her nostrils. When she could breathe again, she tried to fix her hair which was stuck to her face. The sight of Hilary fixing her hair seemed to break Randy's spell and he partially came out of his comatose state. With the unbroken lantern in one hand, Christian got his uncle to break his hold from the fragile pillar.

The slow uphill climb through the passageway lasted nearly an hour. The steady ascent was made more difficult because they had only one light and the bulk of their bodies blocked most of it. Randy struck his head against the rock ceiling several times. In the room at the top they rested for a while, as empty eye sockets stared at them and broken skulls grinned.

"We're almost there," he whispered. "One more tunnel and we'll be back in the sunlight."

A spasm shook Hilary. Randy looked cold, he was trembling.

"I can't."

"Yes you can! Randy, you are *not* going to give up."

Christian searched Randy's pockets while his uncle moaned. He found his Swedish Fish. He opened the bag and put one in Randy's mouth. Randy began to chew, then stopped.

"Chris. Chris. The moon. The moon, it's here."

"Calm down."

Christian stood up and began to pull Randy to his feet, and at that moment the sound of footsteps made him turn his head. A figure appeared in the orb of light. Gary VanCoth was both recognizable and unrecognizable. Their eyes met. Christian could not speak, could not move. This was not a man, it was another kind of life. Something that didn't know *how* to look human. Whatever was inside Gary was so much larger than he was that it spilled out the orifices of his face, giving his head the appearance of a bloated full moon. It gripped Christian by the arms and dragged him kicking and writhing back down into the underworld.

CHRISTIAN STOPPED HIS STORY. A violent crash had rocked the cottage. He heard an immediate sharp series of popping and cracking sounds that sounded like fireworks; the cottage pitched to the side. Pictures tumbled from the walls, tables fell over. The candles he had lit fell onto the coffee table.

"Oh my god." Gloria staggered to her feet. "What happened?"

"Call 911," Christian shouted. He was at the picture window that overlooked the river. When he looked back at Gloria, his face was pale. "An uprooted tree hit the house. The water's too high. I don't think we can get out."

The river had risen 15 feet in the last half hour. The cottage, built on five foot railroad ties, lurched. It felt like the ground had dropped away below them. Outside the dark window, a ghostly white birch tree seemed to move on its own accord. Christian braced himself against the window frame. "We're off the support beams," he told her. He downed his whiskey in a gulp. "They've broke. The house is floating down the river!"

Gloria stared at him for a long second before snatching open her purse. As she groped blindly for her phone, the swirling brown waters of the Susquehanna carried Christian's cottage away.

THEY WERE AT THE MERCY OF THE RIVER. The operator promised a rescue helicopter was on its way. Told Gloria to remain on the phone. The sofa was the only place safe to sit, the only thing not moving, so she sat on it, watching the water come in under the front door.

"I want to hear the rest," she said to Christian, who was kneeling at the window. Her voice shook. There were tears in her eyes. She held her cell phone near her ear. "Finish the story. I'm ready to hear the rest."

Christian's empty glass rolled across the floor. He began.

"It wasn't your husband any more," he told her.

GARY'S BODY LIFTED CHRISTIAN like he was a small child and threw him four feet into the second passageway. He hit the back of his head hard, then was dragged down the steep passage and along the cavern floor to the pit in absolute darkness. Gary's body wrapped its arms around Christian's waist in a terrible embrace, and leapt into the slimy water. It closed over his head, and still he was pulled down into the cold depths.

Cold, bloated worms slid up his body. Christian struggled, his lungs feeling like they were going to burst. He slowly became aware he was floating upwards. He opened his mouth and found he could breathe again. In the pitch darkness he clutched at rocks, a blind struggle half out of the watery slime, kicking wildly at the thing which still grasped his legs. Lacy stone formations cut his fingers as he clawed. The sound of his gasping breath filled the darkness. At the end of the fight to get out of the liquidy mass, Christian was straddling Gary's body on the pits edge. He pressed the thing between his knees and clamped his hands around its throat. It struck Christian fiercely in the ribs and arms but he kept on pressing, seeing its moon face in his mind, and squeezing its throat harder. Even long after the thing's struggles had ceased, he kept his hands locked around its neck.

When Christian finally let go, he crawled ten feet away and, exhausted, sat down. For how long, he didn't know. Then he rose stiffly to his feet and began picking his steps carefully in the dark until his outstretched arms touched vertical rock.

Christian started groping his way toward where he thought the passage was, but his hands met only rock wall. He changed direction, and minutes later found himself in an open area. He rested for a while, then felt his way forward, expecting that at any moment he would touch cold rock. When he didn't, he stopped moving and began to quietly sob, but it was while in the depths of that despair, as total as the darkness around him, that he saw a light. A very small quivering glow, dim red in the darkness in front of him. It rose toward the unseen cavern ceiling, the red light. And then it flexed, permeating the lifeless cavern with a thousand extensions, inhabiting every chamber and subterranean channel like a tortoise within its shell. The crown formation of stalactites became a crown; the red light a lantern. The calcified mummy in the black pool was showing Christian how he was going to die and Christian stared at it, or rather, stared into it, at its blood soul, the red core which bloomed and closed, bloomed then closed again—like a cluster of red butterflies fanning their wings. And saw—believed he saw—because he *hungered* to see—the same color as red Swedish Fish. He had a bag in his coat pocket. He felt to see if it was safe. It was gone, but that was because he had given the bag to Randy. Christian's stomach grumbled.

In a sudden flash, the carnelian light brightened into scarlet. Under it, a figure crawled out of the floor, its movements inhuman. It was Gary, of course, scarlet in the light. It raised itself to a standing position, and then, close behind it, something else rose up out of the crevasse in the cavern floor. Something like a full blood moon.

Christian picked up a broken piece of rock and hurled it as hard as he could. It struck Gary in the face; he fell to his knees. Behind him, the thing that was taller than a man, with a round, bulbous head and a face unlike anything living or anything dead, continued to rise. An impossibly long arm reached across the floor. Five feet to the right of Christian stood the pillar that Randy had refused to let go of. The broken pillar; he could see the series of glowing red cracks. Christian did not think. He hurled himself into the column of bedrock, hit it hard with his shoulder, heard the air whoosh out of him. It gave, breaking into sharp fragments which collapsed in a thunderous slow motion. The great pile of rockfall under his feet began to slide. Christian jumped aside just as it, too, gave away. The contracting and dilating core clinging to the caverns ceiling over his head strove to propel itself downward toward him. Stalactites dropped like thawing icicles. As they fell they took the chambers ceiling with them. A wall crumbled into the pit, burying Gary and the slime filled pit.

The cavern took its last, dying breath.

Christian watched as an arm of sunlight reached down from the destruction and touched upon the sunless place.

THEY STARED AT EACH OTHER in silence for a few moments while the cottage bobbed up and down in the swollen river. Gloria had lifted her feet off the wet rug. She still had her phone near her ear. Christian had switched on a half dozen flashlights and his shadow was dancing on the living room wall.

"I'm sorry, Gloria."

"We said our sorrys a long time ago."

"You were there for the rest," he said. "The room under the mound was intact after the cave-in. Somehow, I got Hilary and Randy out through the hole. When spring came, I filled the mound with dry brushwood and branches and set them on fire. While it was burning, I tried to look into the sinkhole at the edge of the field and I couldn't see anything. But I could smell it. It smelled like rotten earth, a grave, a grave that's Snow land… whenever I smell dirt it reminds me. The dead can never be fully buried. Their bodies are part of the land. Part of the air we breathe. Then, when I went home, I found Randy. He'd had his first stroke." He paused. "And now, here I am."

"Chris, don't give up on yourself. Who knows what the next chapter in your life will bring. You just turned twenty-one, you have your whole life ahead of you."

"No. I'm still a Snow."

"And only you can control your destiny."

"I'm not so sure," he said thoughtfully. Then he turned to her from the window. "Gloria, I see a light outside."

"Oh, Chris! It's the light from the helicopter. It's here to rescue us!"

But it wasn't the helicopter, it was Hilary's car headlights as she was driving across the Bridge Street bridge. Her seven-year-old daughter, going on eight, was in the back seat with Christian's birthday present on her lap, a gift she had made herself. At the mercy of the floodwaters, Christian's cottage listed to one side in the malicious waves, then struck the bridge at 7 mph and was instantaneously smashed apart.

Look for Book Two of the Man in the Moon Trilogy

WINDSOR'S END

IT'S CALLED WINDSOR'S END, a lonely stretch of road at the edge of town, where four families are tormented by dark secrets from the past. But not far above a pale moon is watching... Now, a shadow stirs in Windsor. All over town, in the quiet homes, the stores and taverns, on the streets—fear grows as the lights begin to dim, and Windsor's End is plunged into a terrifying world of endless night.

CPSIA information can be obtained
at www.ICGtesting.com
Printed in the USA
BVOW08s0524240717
489803BV00001B/3/P